THE VICTORIOUS MEETING

A Usurper's War Novella

JAMES YOUNG

Copyright ©2024 by James Young

All rights reserved.

No portion of this book may be reproduced in any form without written permission from the publisher or author, except as permitted by U.S. copyright law.

DEDICATION

To Her Majesty, Queen Elizabeth II

1
NEOPHYTES AND ALLIANCES

Great part of the information obtained in war is contradictory, a still greater part is false, and by far the greatest part is of a doubtful character—**Clausewitz**

H.M.C.S. VICTORIOUS
0345 LOCAL
POINT SUSSEX, INDIAN OCEAN
5 AUGUST 1943

The knocking on the hatch was not particularly loud, but it was very insistent.

I wish I could say I was surprised at that sound, Lieutenant Commander Martin Baines, United States Navy, thought. With a sigh, he opened his eye in the darkened compartment, flicked on the bedside lamp, and reached for his eye patch.

"Just a moment," he called out, trying to keep his annoyance down. The problem with his hosts was that they often had trouble understanding his deep Mississippi drawl, so Martin had to adjust his tone. Some instances worked much better than others. Slipping on the black eye patch, Martin quickly pulled on the pressed, fresh khakis he'd hung up in anticipation of the next few minutes.

Great job being a liaison, Baines thought. *You get to be the person held responsible by men far outranking you in another navy for decisions made by other men who are far superior to yourself in your own navy.*

"Lieutenant Commander Baines..." a voice on the other side began.

"I said, *just a moment*," Baines snapped.

At least this navy speaks the same language, Baines thought, then smiled ruefully. *Or a close facsimile thereof.*

Almost three years after Adolf Hitler's death, *Her Majesty's Royal Navy* and the United States Navy were still working out some minor kinks in their cooperation. Aboard *Her* Majesty's *Commonwealth* Ship *Victorious*, this meant that one Lieutenant Commander Baines was often stuck explaining just why everything the British had worked out with one Vice Admiral William Halsey several months earlier did not carry over to Vice Admiral Jack Fletcher. If he had to guess, the next half hour or so would be a very contentious exercise of that process.

You see, sir, unlike your country, we don't have a sovereign; we have a President, Baines thought angrily. *A man who has been in office too long, but that's neither here nor there. Anyway, since he's not a king, his best efforts to get us involved in* **your** *war failed. Then you guys got your asses kicked by the Germans.*

Baines filled the glass of water by the sink. He took a long swig of it, then looked at his reflection in the mirror to ensure his eyepatch was adequately adjusted to conceal the scars around the missing orb.

Shortly thereafter, because of various actions by the President and the Secretary of the Navy that made little sense to most of the fleet, we somehow ended up fighting the Japanese around Hawaii, Baines thought. *Some of us caught fragments in our eye, and our fleet commander received, if some reports are correct, a Japanese dive bomber to his flag bridge.*

Baines shook his head at the notional conversation he knew he'd never actually be stupid enough to say. The fact of the matter was that the man he was going to see, one Vice Admiral Andrew Browne Cunningham, was well aware of why his counterpart in the Indian Ocean was Vice Admiral Jack Fletcher, not Vice Admiral William Halsey.

Lord knows the damn Royal Navy has enough dead admirals in this war to understand how seniority and brevet promotions work, Baines thought. *Pound. Somerville. Phillips. They're going to start having people cross over to King Edward's side just because they want to see next year, never mind working for some angry teenager.*

Baines allowed himself a wry smile.

And that, my friends, is why I don't drink aboard ship, Baines thought. *Alcohol loosens the tongue and lets the stupid out.* He wasn't quite sure if Vice Admiral Cunningham could have him summarily executed for treason to the British Commonwealth's "rightful sovereign," but the Indian Ocean was a vast place. Baines didn't want to know what happened if one should "fall" overboard.

Besides, of the two people claiming to be the rightful heir to the British throne, Baines mused, *the teenager angry that a bunch of Krauts killed her father has to be a better person by default.* **She** *didn't throw in with a bunch of folks who gassed her capital.*

With that, Baines grabbed a sealed envelope lying under his uniform cap, then opened the hatch to reveal Lieutenant Commander Nigel Farmer, Royal Navy. Like Baines, Farmer was an aviator. Unlike the American, Farmer had both his eyes, even if they looked like icebergs set in a grim, angry expression. The tall, athletic officer appeared as if his rage was barely concerned.

"Figured you'd have sent one of your lieutenants, Nigel," Baines said airily. The British officer's nostrils flared at Baines's confirmation that he'd fully expected a visit at that moment.

"So, you did know that your commanding officer was going off on a lark," Farmer said, referring to Vice Admiral Fletcher. "That after yet another refueling, he moved *away* from Ceylon and off towards the African coast?!"

Baines shrugged. Farmer and he did not exactly have a contentious relationship, but Vice Admiral Cunningham's air officer was well aware Baines had not volunteered for his current position.

Then again, I guess I should just be glad I didn't get invalided out, Baines thought. *Not much use for a former dive bomber pilot with no depth perception.*

"You are aware of how orders work, I assume?" Baines asked, keeping the same calm, indifferent tone he'd had earlier. "Sometimes, when you get message traffic from a seaplane tender, it includes instructions on when you're to reveal certain information. Vice Admirals…"

"*Do not talk to me as if I'm a child, you idiot,*" Farmer shouted. Realizing he'd lost his temper, the British officer closed his eyes and took a deep breath. Baines let Farmer regain control of his emotions and continue.

"I would have considered it a professional *courtesy* if you had maybe given me some type of warning of what was about to happen," Farmer stated. "Both as a fellow aviator and given the *personal* interest I may have in the whereabouts of your fleet elements."

"The fact your brother is aboard one of our heavy cruisers doing the same job I am does not mean I'm about to get myself sent to Kansas for life," Baines replied, then gestured towards the *Victorious'* flag bridge. "Shall we?"

"Kansas?" Farmer asked as they walked. "Why the devil would you be worried about going there?"

"Our military prison is in Leavenworth, Kansas," Baines replied. "Lovely Army town, from what friends have told me, but I doubt it's so charming when you're stuck inside a jail."

Farmer shook his head.

"Well, now that the cat's out of the bag, how about you fill me in before you talk to the old man," Farmer said.

"No," Baines replied simply as they began climbing up the *Victorious'* island.

"What do you mean, no?" Farmer replied. "And how did you bloody well know where we're going?"

"I doubt Captain Mackintosh sent you," Baines replied. "And 'no' is a complete sentence."

He didn't need to turn around to know that Farmer was glaring at him.

"Once again, do orders work differently in this navy?" Baines said without turning around.

Further conversation was cut off by a Royal Navy captain stepping out into the hallway.

So it begins, Baines thought, looking at the man's face. Captain Foote had the great misfortunate of being Vice Admiral Cunningham's flag captain, a position that meant the man was often the first to catch the angry admiral's broadsides. Foote turned to look into the admiral's plot behind him.

"Sir, Lieutenant Commander Baines..."

"Ah, the bloody Americans at last! Send him in; shut the hatch behind you!" Cunningham shouted.

Foote spared Baines a look as the man walked past him. Unlike Farmer, he did not seem to be incensed. Baines nodded at him, then turned the corner.

"You want to tell me what the hell Vice Admiral Fletcher is about?!"

Vice Admiral Cunningham was a tall man with a ruddy face and piercing blue eyes. To an ordinary man in the Royal Navy, Baines was certain that the gaze he received would have been truly intimidating if not bowel-loosening. To Baines, it was simply annoying.

"Sir, I'm going to preface this whole discussion by stating I can give information, or I can be a whipping boy," Baines replied, keeping his tone respectful.

"How dare..." Cunningham began, his face coloring. Baines heard the gasps behind him but charged on.

It's too early in the day to take an ass chewing, and we are short of time.

"Sir, I found out about Vice Admiral Fletcher's plans roughly six hours ago when this force met with the *Curtiss* and her accompanying tankers," Baines continued. "Included in those orders was strict guidance to hold on to the information I was to tell you until *after* the *Curtiss* made her 0300 coded reports to Brisbane for relay to Pearl Harbor."

Vice Admiral Cunningham continued to fix Baines with a furious glare. Baines calmly stared back at him.

Biggest thing you can do with a bully is to let him know he might kick your ass, but you're not going to be a coward, Baines thought. *To be fair, Cunningham is just a hard man, but the same rules apply.*

"Continue," Cunningham said crisply.

"As you may recall, Vice Admiral Fletcher has communicated his concerns with having the Italians to our west and the Japanese to our east," Baines continued. "This concern only increased with your information that two carriers were joining the Italian fleet."

Cunningham snorted.

"Two *carriers?*" the man replied. "The *Dasher* and *Battler* are *hardly* worth disrupting the plan I thought he and I had agreed on for dealing with the goddamn Japanese heading towards Ceylon!"

Yes, well, you haven't had two fleet carriers shot out from under you, Baines thought. *Might change your perspective.* The Battle of Hawaii, in addition to killing the Pacific Fleet's commander and claiming Baines' eye, had also cost the USN the carriers *Lexington, Saratoga*, and *Hornet*. *Lexington* had been serving as Vice Admiral Fletcher's flagship when the Japanese caught that vessel and her sister.

At least **Hornet** *got a chance to get a strike launched before getting seen off*, Baines thought, fighting to keep his face passive as Cunningham continued.

"I am *concerned* at the suitability of a man who seems equally petrified of running out of fuel and a pair of carriers that have less aircraft than just one of his," Cunningham observed acidly. "Perhaps..."

"Perhaps you can take that up with Admiral King," Baines interrupted Cunningham, causing the other man to recoil in shock. "I am but a lowly commander, but I am certain he will inform you exactly how relevant your concerns are to this matter."

"Lieutenant Commander Baines…" Foote began but stopped as Cunningham held up his hand.

"I assume there's a reason you're mentioning Admiral King, Lieutenant Commander?" Cunningham said, his tone cool.

Yep, he's gone beyond anger to simply plotting how quickly he can get me off this vessel depending on what I say in the next five minutes, Baines said. *Good.*

"Admiral King gave Vice Admiral Fletcher explicit orders not to place his force in between two functional hostile forces," Baines stated. "Furthermore, he was directed to eliminate *all* aviation fleet assets pursuant to striking the Italian forces gathering in Somaliland."

Cunningham's eyes narrowed as Baines continued.

"As you can imagine, that's a lot to ask of *Enterprise* and *Yorktown*," Baines stated. "Which is why the Atlantic Fleet has detached the carriers *Bonhomme Richard* and *Independence*, along with the battleships *Massachusetts* and *Indiana*, to Vice Admiral Fletcher's command."

Vice Admiral Cunningham only allowed shock to cross his face for the briefest of instants.

Yes, that's right, the USN just doubled its strength in the Indian Ocean and did not see fit to tell you or anyone in the Royal Navy, Baines thought.

"Well, it would have been nice to know that," Cunningham said after another few moments. "I would have requested that this force regain the *Repulse*."

"I do not believe that anyone was made privy to that information other than those Vice Admiral Fletcher chose to send it to," Baines replied. "If the other communications are to be believed, it is his intent to rejoin this force in sufficient time to affect either *Repulse* rejoining with *Prince of Wales* or the latter being detached to join the other surface heavy ships under Vice Admiral Godfrey."

Baines watched the emotions play over Vice Admiral Cunningham's face.

Yes, that's right, we crazy colonials were talking about putting our vessels under a Commonwealth, admiral, Baines thought. *I can only imagine the conversation **that** led to with Admiral King. Which might explain why he's being such an asshole about cooperating **with our allies**.*

"Why are you risking so much effort in the Indian Ocean?" Cunningham asked. "I had thought your navy's position was that heavy forces could not be spared from a potential thrust to establish bases in the Azores, on Ascension, or retaking Iceland."

From what I hear about the last time we tried to take Iceland, Baines thought, *some of that might be a genuine concern—no thanks to the half of your fleet that's stayed loyal to the Usurper.*

"That was our official position," Baines replied. "Then your forces on Ceylon have made enough of an annoyance of themselves interdicting oil from the Persian Gulf that the Japanese decided to attack in force."

"Thus, your admirals think they can sink enough of them to make it possible to operate in the Pacific," Cunningham observed, visibly calming down. "It would have been nice if you'd informed your friends of this plan."

"Sir, we are informing our friends," Baines said. "Vice Admiral Fletcher could have simply struck Mogadishu in a few hours and left you at a loss where he is. Instead, he had an auxiliary unit broadcast his plans while you still have the ability to adjust yours."

We'll just leave out the fact that it was your folks at Singapore being clumsy with the information that we'd broken the Japanese code that has somewhat caused this lack of distrust between our fleets, Baines thought. *So we're a bit reticent to tell you things anymore.* After the *Luftwaffe* had bombed the British into submission during the Second Battle of Britain, the British were forced to turn over their fortress to the Japanese. Unfortunately, the operation was so haphazard and rushed that many critical papers were not burned.

"Yet he's now too far away for mutual support," Cunningham stated, clasping his hands.

"Yes, and the Japanese have no idea we have doubled our carrier fleet," Baines responded. "So when the Italians comment about hundreds of aircraft over Mogadishu, what are the Japanese going to assume?"

"That this entire force is still on the other side of the Indian Ocean," Cunningham said. A rare grin crossed his face.

"I don't know about you, sir, but I'd probably be quite relieved that my nearest opposition was at least a couple days steaming away," Baines continued. "It might make me assume some risks I may not have otherwise. Why, an enterprising force might be able to sneak up and catch some people by surprise once it's confirmed where they are."

Cunningham looked at Baines with a doubtful expression.

"Let's not be too hopeful," Cunningham replied. "I'll settle for 'otherwise occupied' and giving us a chance to close. Especially since they'll have no land-based air of their own to fly reconnaissance this far into the Indian Ocean."

"Sir, when I went to bed last night, there was only one."

"We have that large Japanese task force our submariners sighted on the 1st," Cunningham said.

"Yes, that is one force," Baines said. "Our fleet intelligence believes they've gotten another that left Brunei just yesterday. Sighted by one of our submarines, but no one's been able to reach her since."

Cunningham pursed his lips.

"It does seem like the Japanese have made an extensive effort to take care of any submarine that sights them," the British admiral replied. "Considering our junior service steadfastly refuses to reassign any heavy bombers from Ceylon to try and find the force that got through the Straits of Malacca, we're not quite sure where the Japanese are."

I suspect they're trying to keep as many of their bombers ready for the main event, Baines thought. The RAF had briefed Vice Admiral Cunningham on what forces were available on Ceylon before the *Victorious* left the Royal Navy's base at

Addu Atoll. Baines thought the man was somewhat distracted at best, wholly out of his depth concerning aviation matters at worst.

Good thing he's got Farmer and an excellent staff.

"Sir, I doubt the Japanese will go unsighted for long," Farmer stated. "We all know where they're going. Between the radar-equipped *Mosquitoes* and *Beaufighters* on Ceylon, we'll likely find them well before they get in range for their aircraft."

Don't be so sure about that, Baines thought bitterly. *Those carrier birds have a longer reach than we realized.*

"I just hope that all these wonder systems you aviators keep telling me about eventually pan out," Cunningham said. "I mean, it's hard enough planning operations with you lot anyway. More so when, apparently, one of my carriers has been crewed by creatures of the night."

*B*IES *O*NE
0445 L*OCAL*

"You know, sir, I don't understand why we didn't just call this kite the *Avenger* like the Americans do," Lieutenant Miles Barker, Royal Canadian Navy, remarked from the *Tarpon*'s middle position. "It's led to nothing but confusion every time we've operated with them, and at this point, it's nothing but sheer stubbornness by our betters."

Commander Servius Ellis, Royal Commonwealth Navy, shook his head at his observer's question.

It is not a bad question, per se, Servius thought as he brought the torpedo bomber into a gentle bank, eyes squinting towards the lightening eastern horizon. *It's just that this would not necessarily be the topic I'd broach while searching for enemy submarines in the middle of the ocean.*

"For not the first time, Miles," Servius said after a moment, "I have no logical answer for your question due to its fundamentally insane nature."

There was a brief chuckle from the *Tarpon*'s belly position.

"Is there something you wish to add, Petty Officer Daniels?" Servius asked, his tone clearly indicating the inquiry's joking nature.

"Oh, sorry, sir, just hiccups," Petty Officer Lucas Daniels replied. "I'll try to avoid hitting the intercom button in the future."

"I mean, just what in the bloody hell were the *Yanks* planning on 'avenging' when they named this aircraft in the first place?" Barker continued. Looking in the rearview mirror, Servius could see the very slight glow of the *Tarpon*'s radar screen.

"You tell me, Barker," Servius replied. "Not being from their continent, I really have no idea what the average Yank thinks about."

"Sir, I'm from Fort St. John, British Columbia," Barker replied. "The closest Yanks to us are technically only Yanks by name only, being from Alaska and all."

There was another long pause, and in his mind's eye, Servius could imagine Barker fussing with the *Tarpon*'s radar set. They were roughly one hundred miles almost due north from the *Illustrious*, with nothing but the featureless ocean beneath them.

Or at least I hope there's nothing but ocean beneath us, Servius thought. *Or we have major problems.*

The nearest enemy forces, at least according to the *Illustrious*' "spooks," were confirmed Italian heavy units at Mogadishu. Task Group 45, as the British carrier contingent was known, was allegedly all by itself at Point Sussex. The area's isolation was the primary reason Vice Admirals Cunningham and Fletcher had chosen it for their tankers.

Still, if one had a pound for every time some enemy showed up where they weren't supposed to be in Royal Navy history, they'd be able to afford a modest cottage in Scotland, Servius thought. *So here we sit, searching the darkness. Hoping nothing goes wrong with an engine manufactured by someone we've never met, in a city we've never been to, and against an opponent we never thought we'd fight.*

"You know what I miss about home?" Barker began. The inquiry led to a groan from the lower turret.

"Gas problems again, Daniels?" Servius asked lightly. "What have I told you about beans before flying?"

"Poutine," Barker said without pause. "I miss good ol' fashion, dripping in gravy poutine."

"Can't say I've ever had poutine," Servius replied. "Personally, I miss a good ol' fashioned Yorkshire pudding."

Servius paused for a moment.

Who knows the next time I'll have one of those, he thought. *There's that little matter of the Germans occupying...erm, 'opening a training facility' near Yorkshire*. Servius was under little illusion as to the relative odds of the Germans being kicked out of England as the war currently stood.

"You're missing out, sir," Barker said. "There's..."

The observer's voice trailed off. There was the sound of items shifting behind Servius.

"What do you have for us, Barker?" Servius prompted.

"Not sure, sir," Barker replied. "I want to make sure we don't have a glitch in the system."

Damn radar has to be one of the most temperamental items I've ever had the misfortune of having to rely on, Servius thought. He scanned his instruments in the cockpit's gloom, ensuring the *Tarpon*'s engine did not indicate any problems.

"What do you have, Barker?"

"Surface contact, bearing oh seven four relative," Barker replied. "Thinking it's at eight miles."

That's the outer limit of the scope for a submarine, Servius thought.

"Signaling Bies Two," Daniels said, referring to the second *Illustrious*-based *Tarpon* flying its own race track pattern just a half mile away.

"Very good," Servius said. "Guess we'll get a chance to see if this new kit the Americans brought over is of any use."

"I'm not sure I trust a torpedo named after a dog," Barker replied.

Fido is a bit of a strange name for a weapon, Servius thought.

But I don't care if it was named 'Dingo.' The thought of a torpedo homing in off sound is insane. Technically dubbed the Mark 24 Mine in an attempt to confuse any potential enemy agents, the new homing weapon had only been in use with the USN for roughly two months. Because of the close relationship enjoyed by the *Victorious*, *Illustrious*, and *Enterprise* due to joint exercises off British Columbia the previous year, the *Illustrious* was gifted sixteen of the weapons.

"Well, beggars can't be choosers," Servius replied.

"Two reports said they've got the contact also," Daniels chimed in. "They're ready to drop flares."

"Very good," Servius replied.

I sincerely hope this isn't some lost American or British submarine, Servius thought suddenly. *That would be a major shame.*

"Daniels, please double-check the daily codes," Servius said.

"MN, DU, and LZ, sir," Daniels responded without pause. Despite the neutral tone, Servius could tell the man did not enjoy being subjected to his squadron commander's doubts.

"Thank you," Servius said.

"Do you honestly think it may be a friendly submarine?" Daniels asked, concerned.

"No, I'm 90% sure it is a hostile submarine," Servius replied. "Assuming it's a submarine and not some neutral merchantman or South African."

"Would certainly be odd this far south," Barker stated. "Please come port five degrees."

Servius skidded the *Tarpon*'s nose. Looking off to starboard, he briefly scanned for Bies Two. After about thirty seconds, he saw the brief spark of flames from the other *Tarpon*'s exhaust.

"Three miles," Barker said.

They've got to hear us by now, Servius thought. *And know that we are getting much closer.*

"Two, this is One," he said, breaking radio silence. "Get the flares out."

"Roger, One. Two starting flare run."

The blue flashes of Bies Two's exhaust brightened momentarily as the other *Tarpon* accelerated. For his part, Servius began to slowly let down in altitude, keeping his eyes on the artificial horizon.

"Bloody hell, contact is starting to fade!" Barker said.

Well, someone spooked, Servius thought, glancing at his airspeed. The FIDO had relatively strict drop parameters. Servius had no desire to break the torpedo just because he'd rushed the delivery.

Good doggo, don't smash up on impact, Servius thought.

"Two is dropping flares."

The night was suddenly very bright in front of Bies One. Unlike the torpedo, flares had no drop restrictions. Servius was glad of that, as it meant the sudden brilliance did not fully blind him. Still, having been airborne for several hours, it took him a moment to gain some semblance of equilibrium.

Looks like that's an I-boat, Servius thought, spotting the submarine's outline. The vessel's deck was still awash, with the conning tower outline and deck gun clearly not German. Servius charged the *Tarpon*'s wing guns.

Best do it now in case this thing blows him back to the surface, he thought. Almost by instinct, borne of many blind drills, he opened the torpedo bay doors. There was the sound of wind inside the aircraft. The submarine's conning tower remained visible as he reached the drop point.

Those propellers should be good and loud, Servius thought. *Come on, Fido, be a good lad*.

"Biers One, dropping!" he radioed, then toggled the weapon. The *Avenger* lifted as it shed a few hundred pounds, and Servius continued forward to overrun the submarine's position.

Always pleasant being in a torpedo bomber when people can't shoot back, he thought. Satisfied he'd gained enough height and that Biers Two was clear, Servius put the *Tarpon* into a gentle climb to port. He glanced back towards the frothing waters where the submarine had disappeared.

. . .

The target for Biers one that evening was the Japanese submarine *I-1*. An older vessel, *I-1* was a cruiser submarine designed for long patrols. Had it not been for the conflict, the submarine would have been headed for the scrapyard by the end of 1944. Given her age, she was slow to dive, not that agile, and noisy underwater. Her captain wisely chose to submerge when he heard the aircraft noises grow louder.

It was the captain's paranoia that caused the submarine to pass fifty feet when the *Fido* hit the water. Rigging for depth charges, the hydrophone operator was the only crew member to hear the torpedo's splash. Realizing what the high-pitched noises in his headphones were, the man screamed a warning across the *I-1*'s control room. In response, the submarine's captain ordered a hard turn to starboard and increased the angle of the dive.

With her engines already rumbling at full speed, the I-boat was unwittingly already as loud a signature as the *Fido* could detect. Turning broadside to the weapon only gave it that much more area to make contact with. Even so, the submarine nearly managed to escape by virtue of descending another ten feet before *Fido* managed to fetch its prey. Not a massive warhead by any means, the roughly one hundred pounds of torpex was still quite capable of punching through the pressure hull.

Going to be hard to tell if we get a hit, I just realized, Servius thought. *Dammit.*

"Ready our flares just in case that damn thing doesn't do its bloody..."

The explosion was a brilliant white light just under the surface, swiftly followed by a disturbance that vomited water up a couple dozen feet. A very subtle rumble was barely audible over the *Tarpon*'s engine.

Christ Almighty, Servius thought. *It must have hit her in the torpedo room.*

"Uh, sir, I think it worked," Daniels said quietly. "At least, I bloody well hope that wasn't what a *miss* looks like."

"I think you just might be right, Daniels," Servius said. "Signal *Illustrious*: Have spotted, engaged, and sunk one enemy submarine, type unknown. Kill definitely confirmed. Fido wags."

Barker laughed from behind the radar scope as Servius looked at his fuel gauge.

We've got enough fuel for another half hour, he thought, listening to Daniels as he typed out the Morse code signal to their home carrier. *Going to be a slight gap between us landing and the daylight ASW, but with those* **Catalina** *seaplanes out beating the bushes things should be fine.*

"I must say, doing that in this kite sure beats the old Stringbags," Barker stated, referring to their old Fairey *Swordfish* biplanes No. 819 squadron had been flying just a few months before.

"Don't need the wind whistling past your ears just to tell you you're alive?" Servius replied.

"No, no, I do not," Barker said. "Just like I don't need to have my fingers numb over the North Atlantic."

I miss home, Servius thought. *Even if it meant freezing our arses off.*

"Well hang around long enough and I'm sure we'll be back that way, sir," Daniels said. "That evil bastard on the throne can't hold out forever."

If only I had the confidence of youth, Servius thought. *No matter, we've got plenty of work to do here.*

H.M.C.S. Ark Royal (Shilling)
1200 Local

"Rakshasa Leader, this is Shilling Base," Flight Lieutenant Venkata Singh's headset crackled. "Please state fuel."

"All right lads, you heard the gentleman," Squadron Leader Malcolm Marshall began. "How are your gauges looking?"

It is truly insane that we are this far from land, Venkata thought, his pulse racing as he put the *Seafire* into a slight turn to follow Marshall into orbit around the Royal Navy task force below. *Yet the **Sunderland** appears to have brought us directly to the carriers.*

The flying boat in question waggled its wings as the six *Seafires* trailing it turned away. Dubbed "The Flying Porcupine" by its opponents, the large aircraft had served as a "navigational assistant" for the half dozen fighters flying from the elderly carrier *Argus*. Nominally Royal Navy aircraft, the *Seafires* were replacements for losses suffered by the *Ark Royal*'s air group. Unfortunately for the "senior service," there were just not enough pilots of its own to go around.

I never thought, in a million years, that I would be attempting to place an aircraft on a ship in the middle of the ocean, Venkata thought. *Whose idiotic idea was it to volunteer for this?!*

"Rakshasa Two, state fuel," Marshall repeated sharply.

Dammit!

"I am at one quarter, Leader," Venkata responded.

"Right, let's keep our head out of the cockpit gentlemen," Marshall admonished. "Two, you're first in the chute."

It is time to see if it's possible to learn how to land on a ship in three weeks, Venkata thought, listening to Marshall inform the *Ark Royal* of their fuel status. *It would be embarrassing to come all this way just to splash into the ocean.*

Looking up, Venkata saw that Marshall was starting the turn for the rest of the flight to begin their orbit to starboard away from the *Ark Royal*. Venkata, for his part, broke out of formation and turned to port to circle into the carrier's landing pattern. To the vessel's starboard, a destroyer began drifting back into the astern position.

Plane guard destroyer, he thought. *Hopefully I don't end up on her, I'll never hear the end of it.*

Glancing up and to his left, Venkata looked over the

family portrait he had affixed to the instrument panel. His father and mother stood beaming in front of their Bombay store, flanked by their five children.

I'm sorry I disappointed you, Father, Venkata thought. *But we can't say we're loyal to the Crown for decades and then suddenly stop just because people claim we're a new nation.* It had been a very lively argument when Venkata opted to remain with the Royal Air Force in the Treaty of Kent's aftermath. His two brothers, both cavalrymen, had decided to join the new, nascent Indian Army. The duo had been sent off to the northwest territories to fight against the rebellious provinces trying to form their own nation called Pakistan.

To think some people wanted the English to decide the partition line, he thought, shaking his head. *I hope those two idiots are all right.*

Lined up in the groove, Venkata pressed the button to drop his wheels. With a soft whir, the *Seafire*'s gear dropped into the airstream. The aircraft immediately began losing speed, but he added a slight amount of throttle to compensate as it closed with the *Ark Royal*.

Just like riding a bicycle, Venkata, he thought. *She's just a **Spitfire** with a hook.*

Looking for the Landing Signal Officer (LSO), Venkata spotted the "batsman" near the *Ark Royal*'s stern. The man stood with his left arm slightly tilted higher than the right, indicating that Venkata's port wing was not quite level. Working with the *Seafire*'s trim tabs, Venkata was pleased to see the man bring his arms level.

*Sink rate good...closure rate good...we're in, we're in...and **cut**!*

The *Seafire* hit firmly, but not too hard, then started jerking to a halt as the arrester hook caught. Venkata waited as the deck crew began their delicate post-landing dance, then followed the instructions on where to taxi his fighter. The entire evolution took under two minutes, and Venkata was climbing out of his aircraft as the next *Seafire* touched down.

Bit chillier than I expected, he thought, the stiff breeze over

Ark Royal's deck hitting the sweat that had accumulated while under the *Seafire*'s glass canopy.

"Welcome aboard the *Ark Royal!*" a voice called from behind the *Seafire*. "I'm Lieutenant..."

The speaker's voice momentarily caught as Venkata removed his flight helmet and scarf.

*Yes, I'm aware it is somewhat surprising to have an Indian pilot crawling out of a **Seafire***, Venkata thought with no ill will.

"I'm sorry, sir, I did not catch your name," Venkata stated, extending his hand. "I am Flight Lieutenant Singh, Her Majesty's Indian Air Force."

The Royal Navy officer extended his hand without hesitation, and Venkata smiled inwardly at that.

Oh good, not an arsehole, he thought.

"Lieutenant Gratham," the Royal Navy officer said. "I'm currently the deputy for No. 806 squadron."

Ah, the poor bastard who has been in charge while waiting on Squadron Leader Marshall, Venkata thought. He glanced around as the ratings began moving his *Seafire* toward the edge of the flight deck.

"Uh, what are they doing?" Venkata asked, trying not to sound alarmed.

Gratham looked over at where the men were pushing, then back at Venkata.

"Don't worry, we didn't have you fly all this way just to shove your fighter over the side," Gratham said with a smile. "They're just putting your kite on an outrigger."

There's so much to learn, Venkata thought, suddenly well aware of his ignorance regarding carriers.

"Why do they put them on outriggers?" he asked.

"Well, keeps the hangar clean for things like maintenance and preparing strikes," Gratham replied patiently. "Also keeps the flight deck clear so we can get the CAP and anti-submarine aircraft cycled."

The RN officer looked perplexed.

"I understand you gentlemen are RAF, but didn't they cover any of this during your training?"

"There wasn't much time to cover beyond the basics of landing on a carrier," Venkata said. "A month ago, I was dancing with Japanese fighters over Darwin."

Terrible time, that, Venkata thought. He'd scored a pair of kills during his time but lost many more friends.

"You'll find that things are a bit more, shall we say, *episodic* out here," Gratham said. "We plastered Madagascar along with the Yanks, then started heading this way when the Japanese pushed through Malacca. Problem is, no one knows where their big carriers are."

"Big carriers?" Venkata asked.

"Yes," Gratham replied. The man looked at Squadron Leader Marshall as he moved to them even while the deck crews were pushing the last of the *Seafire*s towards its cradle.

"If you'll excuse me," Gratham said. "I think that is the man I've been sent to snag."

"Yes, of course," Venkata replied. He watched as Gratham went to meet up with Marshall.

"Sir, no disrespect, but if you stand there you will be cursed at by the air boss," a deck rating said, gesturing back towards the island. "If you grab the rest of your lot, I'll have someone show you to the ready room."

"Yes, let me get the other pilots," Venkata thought. He watched as a stocky, radial engine aircraft was being pushed into position.

"What is that aircraft?" he asked.

"*Gannet*," the deck crewman said. "The Americans call it the *Hellcat*."

Venkata watched as the aircraft unfolded its wings, looking for all the world like an awakening raptor.

"Clear the flight deck!" a loudspeaker boomed. "I say again, *clear the bloody flight deck!*"

"That would be the air boss!" the rating stated. "I'd move smartly, gentlemen."

Venkata looked at the gathered pilots as they shuffled towards the ready room.

Welcome aboard, indeed, he thought.

. . .

Twenty minutes later, Venkata felt slightly less sure he was not making a grave mistake.

"So, to recap, you gentlemen will be folded into No. 806 Squadron," Commander Hunter Phillips, *Illustrious* air group commander, explained to the gathered officers. "Squadron Leader Marshall will become the squadron leader, while the surviving members will task organize."

Sounds like that was one hell of a bounce, Venkata thought. Apparently, No. 806 Squadron had been flying top cover for the strikes on Madagascar a few short days before. Unbeknownst to the eight *Seafires*, a German *Gruppen* of Fw-190s had recently been assigned to the island to cover the French-Italian ships stationed there. Expecting only French pilots flying obsolete Curtiss *Hawks* and some older French aircraft, the Royal Navy pilots were somewhat less attentive.

At least Commander Phillips is honest about it, Venkata thought. *Happens to anyone, just not usually to the tune of six lost fighters.*

"Sir, how will fighters be assigned?" Flying Officer Harris, a fresh-faced Australian who'd only had his wings for about eighty days, asked. There was a groan from someone behind Venkata.

You know, there's no reason to be an arse about an honest question, Venkata thought. Harris slightly colored as Phillips spared the offending pilot a glare.

"Seniority," Phillips said. "Thanks to the air sea rescue efforts of our American friends, *Leftenant* Duncan got pulled out of the water so he could forget his manners here."

Well that's an odd way to do it, Venkata thought. *So potentially Harris flew all the way out here just to be a spare pilot?* Apparently Duncan and one other pilot were rescued by an American submarine, transferred to one of their *Catalinas*, and brought back to the *Ark Royal* the day before.

"Don't worry, everyone in here will get a chance to fly," Phillips said. "Although not as strict about crew rest as our

American friends, I assure you there's been vigorous discussions about the need to rotate pilots before we end up in a carrier battle."

I guess I'll have to get one of the Royal Navy blokes to explain that last bit, Venkata thought. *Not that we RAF folks are exactly good about not trying to fly people into the ground. Literally.*

"Now, I think that I'm keeping you gentlemen from the galley," Phillips stated. "So if you'll excuse me, I'll turn you over to Squadron Leader Marshall."

Marshall stood as Phillips walked out the hatch. Venkata watched as the squadron's new commander stood at the front of the ready room. Out of the corner of his eye, he also saw Gratham staring at his new commander.

"Okay gentlemen, you heard Commander Phillips," Marshall said. "I know some of you are hoping to have a go at the Japanese when the time comes. I'm sure there will be plenty of opportunity to go around. For now, let's get some food and meet back here in thirty minutes. Dismissed."

The gathered pilots all stood at that, waiting for Marshall to leave. As he was walking out, Venkata heard a voice mutter from the back of the compartment.

"You know things are bad when we've got a bunch of crabs aboard."

Venkata paused in the hatch.

"I'm certain it's not the first time some of you have had crabs in your organization," he observed over his shoulder. With that, he stepped out of the ready room and onto the gallery deck. Looking across the hangar, Venkata saw the first of the half dozen *Seafires* being lowered down from the flight deck.

"It would appear that someone botched the paint job," Gratham said.

"Sir?"

"Only supposed to be one roundel, not one on each wing," Gratham replied. "Oh well, at least they got all the red out of the center."

Venkata looked at the *Seafire*, then turned to look at the RN officer.

"You really think someone would mistake that small bit of red in our official roundel for a Japanese rising sun?"

"Have you met a Yank?" Gratham replied. "They are extremely trigger-happy."

Venkata shook his head.

"Yes, as a matter of fact, I have, sir," he replied. "I see nothing wrong with your assessment."

IMPENETRABLE PLANS...

Let your plans be dark and impenetrable as the night, and when you move fall like a thunderbolt—**Sun Tzu**

H.M.C.S. ILLUSTRIOUS
ADDU ATOLL
0300 LOCAL
9 AUGUST

There was a long, poignant pause in the *Illustrious'* radio shack as two of the *Illustrious'* squadron leaders and her air group commander looked at one another. They had just read a coded message, sent from Ceylon, informing Task Force 45 of three things. First, the missing Japanese fleet had not only been sighted, but was now apparently less than five hundred miles from Ceylon. Second, the land-based *Mosquito* and *Beaufighter* aircraft based on Ceylon had attempted a strike against the distant Japanese fleet. Third, said strike had led to the loss of almost half of the RAF bombers.

"Out of professional courtesy, I will not comment on the idiocy of sending a bunch of crabs out on an overwater mission," Lieutenant Commander Xavier McGee, No. 885 Squadron's commander, stated.

"That would be prudent," Servius said, attempting to keep his voice level. McGee looked at him in surprise.

You've been an ass pretty much since we got out here to the Indian Ocean, Servius thought. *Even if your squadron has done a fair job of picking off shipping.* Whereas Servius' squadron primarily focused on the anti-submarine mission, McGee's *Tarpons* had feasted on several Axis vessels in and around Madagascar during the Allied raid on that island.

"I knew their squadron leader," Servius continued. "Pleasant chap. Got much of his squadron through the Dutch East Indies campaign. They punched above their weight class in that fight."

Servius looked at his copy of the decoded message and felt a wave of sadness.

"Our entire effort is diminished by these losses."

The subsequent pause was awkward as Servius kept reading. The *Illustrious'* engines began to throb louder as the carrier completed her transition through the mined channel just outside the atoll's main anchorage.

Sure hope that the chaps ashore are up to the task of keeping the I-boats away from the entrance, Servius thought briefly. In the two nights since his own kill, the rest of No. 819 Squadron had dropped ordnance on at least three more submarine contacts. Like Servius' target, one had very obviously been a *Fido*'s second kill. The other was attacked with more conventional depth charges, results unknown.

If the enemy was trying to set up a picket line, we certainly cut some hunks out of the fence, Servius thought with some pride. *We'll see if it holds up.*

After two minutes in which Servius could feel Xavier's eyes still upon him, the *Illustrious'* air group commander, Commander Trevor Lovejoy, diplomatically cleared his throat.

"What do you think of this reported use of Cat's Eyes' fighters in conjunction with what may have been rudimentary radar direction?" Lovejoy asked once Servius looked up.

"I think that could be a problem when we finally get

within range," Servius stated. "This entire night air group concept has been predicated on us *Tarpon*s not needing fighter escort."

"I still don't think we will," McGee snapped. Realizing he had made a misstep when Lovejoy fixed him with a glare, McGee quickly modulated his tone while continuing. "It says in the report, albeit an early one, that the fighters were ineffective."

"Except you'll also note that they definitively confirmed Squadron Leader Russell's death was to an enemy fighter," Servius replied. "That was a *Mossie* and they still caught it. Doesn't lend itself to our *Tarpons* having a good day unless we're very careful."

"He has a point," Lovejoy said, cutting McGee off before the man could argue further. "What are you thinking as a possible solution?"

"If we make a night strike, as Vice Admiral Cunningham has alluded to, we work our way around to the far side of the formation," Servius stated. "They'll be expecting *Mosquitoes* or *Beaufighters* coming in at high altitude from Ceylon."

If we get up there in time, Servius thought. *Those American idiots heading to Somaliland didn't help matters much.*

"Sir, how sure are we about the ship identification?" McGee asked.

"As sure as anyone can be in the dark with a bunch of searchlights trying to blind you," Lovejoy stated. "Which is to say not at all, but we're not getting paid to second guess."

Which is all well and good, as I wouldn't relish someone trying to convince Vice Admiral Cunningham that maybe we should just wait for the Americans to join us here before heading north, Servius thought. He'd been surprised when the *Illustrious* had started shifting in her anchorage.

"So if there are five carriers as the crabs suspected," McGee began, "how are we attacking?"

"I think Servius has the right of it and that we should work our way around to the Ceylon side," Lovejoy replied. "If we can maintain the element of surprise, we should be all right."

There was a peal of thunder, the *boom* making all three of them jump. A moment later, they heard the hard pittering of rain on the *Illustrious*' deck.

Looks like we won't be sending out any anti-submarine aircraft tonight, Servius thought. *And I am very, very glad for that if we're going to be launching a strike the night after.*

"Does anyone have any bloody idea where the Americans are?" McGee asked. "Any at all?"

"I don't know," Lovejoy said. "After they beat up the Italians and sank the *Dasher* and *Battler*, they went back to radio silence. Rear Admiral Vian's staff estimates they'll join us sometime tomorrow."

"Going to be interesting how our opponents deal with *eight* carriers," McGee replied gleefully. "Especially with us able to strike at night."

Problem is, our opponents are like the Americans, Servius thought. *Cram as much aircraft, petrol, and ammunition into a wood tinderbox, then hope you get off the first punch. Illustrious*, on a good night and with perfect mechanical preparation, no other responsibilities, and favorable winds, could put between 24 and 30 *Tarpon*s off her deck. That was the realistic extent of her offensive capabilities. One of the American or Japanese carriers, with those same conditions, could launch over twenty each fighters, bombers, and torpedo bombers toward their prey.

Of course, again, if you so much as hit them with a single bomb at the wrong time, Servius thought, *it will look like the 5th of November. Indeed, Guy Fawkes could only hope to have initiated such a display.* Although he'd not actually seen an American carrier hit, Servius had been around enough Battle of Hawaii survivors to hear how the *Lexington* and *Saratoga* had been set ablaze.

When you can see the smoke from your fleet anchorage allegedly, Servius thought grimly. *Although I think that was a bit of exaggeration or someone conflated the flames and smoke from the Yank battle line.*

"I just wish we could ditch the *Warspite* and *Malaya*," McGee said, referring to the two *Queen Elizabeth*-class battleships that were now part of the *Illustrious'* task force. "We're going to get left behind if our scouts find the Japanese before the Americans do. Vice Admiral Cunningham is not a patient man."

Vice Admiral Cunningham is too much of a destroyer man, Servius thought. *It shows at times like this.* Their commander was infamous for being an expert with small ships, middling with large ships, and mostly lost when it came to properly employing airpower.

To be fair, it's not like the Americans have done a bang up job with it, Servius mused. *Indeed, so far the only folks who have been quite effective have been our friends we're going to go see.* That thought gave him pause as he continued the conversation.

"If it comes down to a fight of us versus the Japanese alone, you'll be glad for the extra antiaircraft help," Servius remarked. "Even if I'm not sure *Malaya* will be so much help as an additional target."

"That's rather cynical," McGee scoffed.

"He's not wrong," Lovejoy replied grimly.

If Vice Admiral Syfret keeps a couple of those damnable Japanese aircraft from putting torpedoes into this ship, it'll probably be a net gain, Servius thought. The *Malaya* was ancient as battleships went. It had only been due to her assignment to the lesser Eastern Fleet that she'd been able to flee to Australia after the Treaty of Kent. Which was a shame, as her crew would have been put to far better use elsewhere.

*Still, armor and guns are armor and guns. Don't want to end up like **Glorious** if some Japanese surface group somehow gets up close with us.*

"Come daylight, I'm pretty sure we'll have a better picture," Lovejoy said, looking at the clock. "For now, go get some rest and sleep. We'll see what the evening brings tomorrow."

H.M.C.S. Victorious' Admiral's Office
0900 Local
Indian Ocean

"As much as it pains me to do so, Lieutenant Commander Baines," Vice Admiral Cunningham said, waving a message flimsy in his hand, "I must congratulate Vice Admiral Fletcher on his thoroughness."

The man's been positively a ray of sunshine compared to the last couple of days, Baines thought as he finished entering Cunningham's "office." Usually a compartment set up so that the Admiral could deal with the massive amount of administrative trivia that often beset a major command, currently the space was dominated by a large map of the northern Indian Ocean. Several small miniature vessels, in various state of painting and upkeep, were stationed around Ceylon. Baines recognized them from various training aids he'd seen scattered about the *Victorious*' ready rooms and intelligence shack.

"Sir, I'm afraid I don't follow?" Baines said. "The last I'd heard, Vice Admiral Fletcher was maintaining radio silence."

With 'last I heard' meaning yesterday when you were screaming at me about my idiotic boss, Baines thought silently. He heard Farmer's intake of breath behind him, but Cunningham ignored the pointed reminder.

I really need to see about getting reassigned, Baines thought. *I'm going to give Farmer a heart attack, even if his boss seems to like combative subordinates. That is, provided they know their shit.*

"Without getting into how we received the information," Cunningham replied, "let's just say it's been confirmed that your forces sank the *Dasher* and *Battler*."

The Vice Admiral looked past Baines at Farmer.

"My apologies to anyone whose colleagues may have been aboard," the senior officer said. Baines could see the man's regret was genuine. "They also seemed to have bagged the cruiser *Sussex*, so no doubt all of us will be mourning friends soon."

"Civil wars are terrible things, sir," Baines observed. "It is a crying shame that our two great navies are forced to do this to one another."

"Thank you, Lieutenant Commander," Cunningham said with a solemn nod. "Also, it is regretful that it appears the *Littorio* and *Giulio Cesare* both escaped to Mombasa."

Baines racked his brain trying to remember what vessels Cunningham was talking about. The Italian Fleet had never really been a concern of his, being a lifelong Pacific Fleet officer.

"Consider this a retraction of all the horrid things I've been saying about Vice Admiral Fletcher these last couple of days," Cunningham continued. "As someone who spent a good year or so trying to bring the Italian fleet to battle, I understand why he may have had concerns. I wish he had not found out firsthand just how fast their vessels are."

Clearly he knows more about this engagement than I do, Baines thought. His confusion must have been evident, as Cunningham made a waving gesture toward the table.

"I'm sure things will reach you through your channels soon enough," Cunningham said. "The real reason I called you in here was recent conversations with my staff have made me realize just how deficient I am in understanding what went wrong for your navy off Hawaii."

Baines hoped his anger only briefly flashed over his face.

*What went "wrong" was about ten years of stupid politicians and the fact **your** government let the Japanese know we'd broken their codes*, Baines thought. Once more, Cunningham read him like a book.

"This is not a second guess or a desire to..." the man paused, then forged ahead with the idiom, "...open old wounds."

Thanks, Admiral. They're not actually all that old, Baines thought uncharitably. *At least, judging from the foreign objects that keep making their way to the surface now and again.* He tried to keep his face expressionless as Cunningham continued.

"It is a matter of knowing my own shortcomings."

The admiral nodded towards Farmer, who had stepped from behind Baines and to the left.

"Officers such as Lieutenant Commander Farmer have tried to educate me with varying degrees of success," Cunningham stated. "However, I will freely admit up until your force came to grief off of Hawaii, I did not believe torpedo aircraft could seriously threaten an underway battleline. Smaller vessels, yes, but not battleships."

Always glad to find out I was part of a thought-altering lesson. Baines inwardly scoffed. He forced his anger and bitterness away as he realized Cunningham was genuinely groping for answers.

"Our service neglected its air element," Cunningham stated. "The reasons for that are voluminous and useless to this discussion. Your country has been gracious in allowing us to acquire several of your aircraft. I am now asking you, Lieutenant Commander Baines, to help me in using them effectively."

Baines thought for a moment, chewing the inside of his cheek.

"Sir, the first mistake we made was not immediately launching a Combat Air Patrol before dawn," Baines said after a moment. "We believed the Japanese were far, far out of range on the other side of the Pacific."

Cunningham nodded as Baines continued.

"The second mistake was keeping the carriers all together," he allowed. "Maybe someday we'll figure out how to properly direct our fighters like y'all have, but things were a mess that day."

"So you do not subscribe to your fellow countrymen's theories on concentration?" Cunningham asked.

"Sir, you need a lot more fighters per carrier for that to be effective," Baines stated. "If someone is throwing his Sunday punch at you, you'll need something solid to block it with. At

Hawaii, we didn't get enough fighters up in time, even with seeing the second Japanese wave coming."

Baines closed his eye for a second, thinking back to that day.

Didn't help that our damn commander was more interested in proving a point about readiness than acting like someone who was going to fight a fleet action, Baines thought. *I really do hope he died doused in gasoline.*

"Failing something to block with, the best option is to make hitting you harder for him than it will be if everyone is gathered together in one nice group," Baines continued. "Sure, he's going to smash the hell out of the small group he finds, but in turn that means you're going to get to catch *all* of him."

Cunningham nodded at Baines' statement. Looking over at his flag secretary, the vice admiral began to give orders.

"Signal the *Illustrious* and *Ark Royal* to stop attempting to close with this force," Cunnigham said. "They are to keep ten miles separation and maneuver independently for now."

"Yes sir," the flag secretary replied, scribbling notes.

"Sir, we don't have enough fighters to maintain the strongest of CAPs," Farmer stated. "Perhaps we should place a picket in front of the force. A radar equipped one."

Cunningham looked at the map in front of him.

"Perhaps something to plan for this evening with the whole staff," he stated. "I don't want to do something rash and get a bunch of cruisers and destroyers sunk."

I suspect they'd appreciate that, Baines thought. *Plus you guys don't exactly have a lot of ships left.* The Treaty of Kent had split the Royal Navy. Those vessels abroad and the others that had broken out along with the Royal Family remained loyal to Queen Elizabeth. Unfortunately, that had been chiefly older capital vessels, even if most were refitted during the nine-month lull between Hitler's death and the resumption of hostilities. Baines looked briefly over at the portrait with a black ribbon around its brown edges hanging in the corner of the compartment.

Well Mr. Churchill, you were proven right once again, Baines thought. *Even if I understand everyone believed you were crazy for continuing to spend money at a wartime pace.*

"I do wonder what he would have thought about all this also," Cunningham said, causing Baines to jump in surprise. "I looked forward to telling him he was right about the Japanese heading to Ceylon several months ago."

Baines shook his head.

"I feel I must once again apologize for my countrymen, sir," he stated. "No one should be trying to kill a young lady, regardless of her status."

Cunningham gave a grim smile at that statement.

"Alas, people killing children in order to confirm usurper's rights to a throne play far too prominent a place in our history," Cunningham replied. "I am only glad that Prime Minister Churchill was there to defend Her Majesty. He and I had several sharp differences during my time as Mediterranean Fleet commander, but we both served the Crown."

Stupid American Bund members, Baines thought. *I hope Hoover and the G-men are rounding them up and shooting them out of hand.* From what little bit that had reached the task force, it had appeared that roughly ten members of the American Bund had attempted to kill Her Majesty as she was traveling across Pennsylvania. They had failed, but only because Winston Churchill had apparently shielded Queen Elizabeth with his body.

"But back to the matter at hand," Cunningham said. "What else should I know before we run into the Japanese tomorrow?"

Baines was about to answer when the sound powered phone on the bulkhead buzzed. Cunningham's secretary looked at a young ensign who'd been previously reading an intelligence bulletin. The young officer sprang up then walked over to the device, the room's eyes on him. There was a quick conversation that Baines followed only part of.

Bit early for CAP to be engaging enemy aircraft, isn't it? he thought nervously. He looked at his watch.

"Sir, one of *Eagle*'s *Sea Hurricanes* reports engaging an enemy seaplane roughly forty-five miles from the task force," the ensign stated, referring to the older carrier accompanying *Victorious*.

Cunningham's eyes narrowed.

"And?"

The young officer looked sheepishly at the vice admiral.

"That is all, sir," the young man replied. "Apparently the weather north of here is playing havoc with the radio, and *Eagle* did not want to break silence to get clarification."

"That bloody idiot," Cunningham muttered.

Which bloody idiot? Baines thought, then realized Cunningham might not know himself.

"Big difference if that's a single engine seaplane or one with four," Farmer commented.

Cunningham looked at the map.

"How in the bloody hell would a single engine seaplane be this far out, Lieutenant Commander Farmer?" Cunningham asked. Baines realized his tone was more vexed than disbelieving.

Farmer looked pensive for a moment.

"I guess that does defy the location of the sighting report," Farmer replied. "Or the current reports out of Ceylon regarding carrier aircraft attacking. So it must be one of their four engine jobs.

Baines thought for a moment.

"Haven't we been experiencing a great deal of submarine activity the last three days?" he asked.

The British officers all turned to look at him.

"I'm failing to see the relevance, Lieutenant Commander Baines?"

"Well, the Japanese have seaplane carrying submarines," Baines replied. "If they pushed their submarines far to the south, this could be one of those aircraft."

"Hmm," Cunningham thought. "Not sure I like the

thought of those submarines sounding a warning that we're coming."

Baines smiled.

"Well, sir, one way to solve that problem is to increase the anti-submarine patrols," he said.

"Agreed," Farmer stated. "Especially as, if I remember correctly, those submarines have to stay on the surface to recover the seaplanes."

"Yes," Baines stated. "Or else their crews are going to have a very long sit in an empty aircraft."

"Given what the weather's been doing for the last twenty-four hours, I'm not sure I'd want to be alone in a bloody seaplane without a mothership," Farmer noted.

"So to be clear, you gentlemen are suggesting we start launching more aircraft for search?" Cunningham asked.

"Yes, sir," Farmer and Baines said, almost in unison.

"Very well," Cunningham stated, looking over at his secretary.

"Sir, recommend we use the battleship and cruiser aircraft," Farmer said.

"No," Cunningham immediately replied. "Takes too bloody long to launch and recover the seaplanes, especially with the weather expected to get worse later today."

That is true, there is that front bearing down from the northeast, Baines thought. He looked at the array of models on the map. *Makes me slightly happier we've got the **Prince of Wales** with us. Add in **Warspite** and **Malaya** and there's at least enough gunpower to hold off a Japanese force long enough to get a strike launched.*

"I need to know what that *Sea Hurricane* pilot saw as soon as he lands, understand?" Cunningham stated.

"That storm front is playing hell with the electronics, sir," one of Cunningham's staff noted. "We've had a couple of false echoes from the lightning in it."

I really hope those are false echoes, Baines thought. *If I recall, the Japanese also have those seaplane cruisers that are all guns up front and nothing but aviation handling in the back.*

He looked at the map once more.

Be nice if the folks up at Ceylon could tell us if they've seen those two ships.

"Let's be about our planning, gentlemen," Cunningham stated, breaking Baines out of his own thoughts. Pushing thoughts of Japanese seaplane cruisers from his mind, Baines started paying attention to Cunningham as the vice admiral dispensed guidance.

H.M.C.S. Ark Royal (Shilling Base)
1200 Local

"So to recap, if it's the *Zero*, do **not** turn with them," Squadron Leader Marshall finished, once more tapping the aircraft recognition poster behind him. "Especially in a *Martlet*."

Over half of the *Ark Royal*'s fighter pilots were gathered in an impromptu classroom at the hangar room's front. Behind them, a group of mechanics worked on a *Tarpon* while another couple toiled away on an aforementioned *Martlet* hauled down from storage.

Three different types of fighters on one vessel has to be a maintenance nightmare, Venkata thought. He was not sure who was to blame for the dismal state of Fleet Air Arm's acquisition process, but the fruits of that idiocy were on full display down the hangar. At the rear, a handful of *Tarpon* torpedo aircraft were being readied for their rotation in anti-submarine duties. Forward of them, the remaining *Seafires* from *Ark Royal*'s original contingent were being refueled and rearmed for their turn on CAP. The carrier's *Gannets* were already airborne, helping form the inner protective wing around the *Ark Royal* and *Illustrious*.

Not quite sure if I like this concept of a "duty carrier," Venkata thought. *Then again, it means we get to fly more often.* He knew his own fighter was fully fueled and waiting for him to take off in another twenty minutes for his turn orbiting above the carrier off Marshall's wing. After the last three days, all of the new arrivals had started to get comfortable coming back aboard a postage stamp in the ocean.

I can understand why the FAA thought it prudent to have multi-seat fighters, Venkata mused as Marshall changed the poster on the easel. *I imagine it is frighteningly easy for the chaps that have to fly out of visual distance to get lost coming back to this vessel.*

He briefly glanced back to where a pair of *Fulmar*s were suspended from the hangar roof.

Still, if what the old hands say about that "fighter" is true, I'd rather take my chances of possibly flying out into nothingness than get caught in a slow, heavy beast like that against one of these Japanese types.

"Given the Americans' propensity to assign code names to everything," Marshall began, "this fighter is called a 'George.'"

There was a collective muttering around the gathered pilots.

"Yes, I know, but we suffer our allies' habits in silence," Marshall continued, drawing polite laughter from the group as he continued. "I promise you, if you think their Navy chaps are weird, try flying with their Army chaps."

Venkata saw several of the RN officers look at one another in puzzlement.

I wish he was being facetious about the Army and Navy folks being a different breed, Venkata thought. He had yet to interact with any American naval officers. However, in working with the American Army, he knew just how much the two services *loathed* one another. In ways that were, to Venkata at least, quite unhealthy.

"In any case, this is another radial engine kite," Marshall continued. "Four 20mm cannons, excellent roll rate, and faster than anything on this carrier."

Marshall's eyes swept the gathered pilots.

"Of course, it doesn't have the best turn rate when compared to the *Seafire*," he stated. "It's about equal to the *Gannet*'s. Also, while not as prone to catch fire as the *Zero*, it isn't exactly stubborn about it."

Venkata found himself nodding in agreement to the comment about the *Zero*. Both of his kills had been of the Japanese fighter. One had been shooting an aircraft off of Marshall's tail. The other was during a surprise bounce when radar had put them in position. In each case, turning both aircraft into flaming comets only took a short burst.

*The **Spitfire** has its issues,* Venkata thought. *But thankfully helping pilots' families save on their funeral pyre is generally not one of them.*

"The Americans took a drubbing from the..."

Marshall was cut off from continuing his statement by the *Ark Royal*'s Tannoy.

"Action Stations, Action Stations, all hands to Action Stations!"

The pilots all looked at each other briefly, then as one began breaking for respective stations.

"Singh, with me!" Marshall shouted, gesturing towards the ladder upwards. Venkata followed his squadron leader up to the flight deck. Four *Seafires* were already arrayed aft, their pilots aboard. Marshall looked like he fleetingly considered running for one, but their engines began turning over before he could start the action. Instead, he grabbed one of the running flight deck officers.

"What's going on?" he asked.

"Radar's just picked up a big bloody raid headed this way!" the man replied. "Coming from the northeast!"

"What?" Marshall asked.

"Gotta go, mate!" the officer replied, shrugging out of Marshall's grasp and running down the flight deck.

"All personnel clear the flight deck! All personnel clear the flight deck!"

Venkata looked at where a crew began to wrestle one of the *Seafires* off the outrigger. He turned back to see Marshall rushing towards the closest aircraft, the deck crew similarly working on getting the aircraft ready for launch.

Are we sure it's the Japanese? Venkata thought, stunned. Gazing in the offending direction, he saw nothing but a dark wall of cloud. There was the roar of engines as a flight of fighters headed off in that direction. Turning back to the direction the *Ark Royal* was heading, Venkata saw a much thinner squall in front of the carrier.

Lucky for us that squall is there, he thought. *Even if it means someone might be taking off in the rain.*

The first *Seafire* roared down the flight deck behind him. The shark-nosed fighter was barely past the end of the flight deck and turning towards starboard before the next fighter began its launch.

No time to sit here like an idiot, he thought. The third *Seafire* was taking off by the time he reached the outrigger. The group of deckhands stood around the aircraft.

"What can I do to help?" he asked the petty officer. The man looked him up and down, then realized the person standing before him was a pilot.

"Sir, you can help push," the man said. Venkata got into position to do just that as the fourth and last *Seafire* that had been previously spotted finished its takeoff run.

"All right you lot, let's go or we'll be swimming in a few minutes!" the petty officer shouted. With that, Venkata helped the deckhands pull the *Seafire* off the outrigger then onto the flight deck. He could see Marshall's aircraft get wheeled into position as his flight crew was about halfway down the flight deck.

"Faster you dolts! Faster!"

Venkata heard a sound like distant thunder. Looking off the *Ark Royal*'s starboard quarter, he saw the *Victorious* with smoke pouring from her funnel as she accelerated. The battleship *Prince of Wales* was similarly accelerating and turning to place herself to the *Victorious'* starboard quarter.

"Sir!" the petty officer shouted. Venkata turned back to see the group had moved on twenty feet in the time he was gawking.

Maybe they'll miss us, Venkata thought. *That is a pretty horrible storm.*

3

...AND FALLING THUNDERBOLTS

And the fellow died as he lived, but it is part of a sailor's life to die well—**Stephen Decatur, USN**

H.M.C.S. V*ictorious*
*1245 L*ocal
I*ndian* O*cean* N*ortheast of* A*ddu*
*9 A*ugust

"The CAP is making contact now, sir."

Baines was not sure who made the report, focusing on the clouds astern of the *Victorious*. There were suddenly flashes inside of the clouds that were clearly not lightning, with balls of flame descending out of the forward side of the storm.

Probably a few collisions in that murk, Baines thought, trying to focus on anything but the cold ball of fear inside his chest. *I personally would have waited for the Japanese to come out of the cloud, but I'm just a dumb dive bomber pilot.*

"What's the likely count?" Cunningham asked, his expression tight.

"At least a hundred enemy aircraft, sir," Farmer said, his face ashen.

"I'm guessing the CAP won't be able to hold at ten-to-one odds?" Cunningham asked, his glasses still to his face.

"No sir, unlikely," Farmer replied.

"The *Ark Royal* and *Illustrious* are into the squall, sir."

Baines looked at Cunningham as he nodded to indicate he'd heard. The air battle was moving swiftly towards *Victorious*, dark dots starting to circle towards starboard and port as they descended. Unable to stare at approaching doom, Baines looked over the British formation around the carrier. Three destroyers steamed in a semicircle ahead of their larger charge, smoke starting to pour from their stacks as well as chemical generators astern. To starboard, the heavy cruiser *Frobisher* kept pace with the *Victorious*. On the opposite side from the *County*-class cruiser was the carrier *Eagle*, with the light cruiser *Emerald* off the much older carrier's port side. Astern of both carriers, the *Prince of Wales* stood ready to lend her anti-aircraft battery to the carriers' short range defense. Four more destroyers, evenly spaced down either side of the formation, rounded out the screen.

It's not going to be enough, Baines thought. *Not going to be anywhere near enough.* He'd seen just how expert and determined the Japanese carrier group attacks were. While Baines had no idea how the Japanese force had seemingly teleported the night before from the position they were reported at, he knew that one hundred aircraft was almost certainly enough to inflict grievous harm to the British formation.

"Lieutenant Commander Baines, stop looking like we're at a funeral," Vice Admiral Cunningham barked. "We'll be fine; she's one of the stoutest carriers in the fleet."

Baines looked at Cunningham, then the deploying Japanese aircraft.

We'll just have to agree to disagree, sir, he thought.

There was great cause for Baines' concern. The Japanese escort had neutralized the majority of the CAP. Getting in position a few thousand yards off of *Victorious*' starboard quarter, Commander Mitsuo Fuchia of the carrier *Akagi* began to direct the 45 dive and 55 torpedo bombers amongst those vessels he could see. As the lead punch of the Japanese *Kido Butai*, or "First Air Fleet," as their six carriers were called, the pilots were all highly experienced. It gave most of them confidence to finally come to blows with the Royal Navy.

The first to open fire was the *Prince of Wales*. With the Japanese force splitting up to approach their targets from astern, the battleship's secondary began firing. Baines watched with professional interest and rising terror as the British anti-aircraft fire attempted to do what the CAP could not. Moments later every ship in the task force joined *Prince of Wales*, the skies suddenly dark with anti-aircraft shells exploding.

Brave fuckers, Baines thought as first one, then another, dive bomber burst into flames and fell out of the formation.

"It would appear that deck is going to get a workout today," Farmer shouted over the din. Baines felt nowhere near as sanguine about the matter as his Royal Navy companion did.

Those are about to be 1,000-lb bombs falling, friend, he thought. *I don't care how armored her deck is, that's not going to end well.* The next weapons to open fire were the 40mm pom-poms, the rapid fire weapons throwing tracers up towards the dive bombers reaching their pushover point.

Wonderful thing about being the target is you don't have to worry about deflection, Baines thought, watching as the first Japanese bomber pushed over. Then he was bracing himself as *Victorious*' captain ordered her into a sharp turn.

"Bloody hell, the torpedo bombers have an almost free run!" Farmer shouted, pointing. Baines turned to see that his British counterpart was right, the poor *Victorious* having bombers off both bows. It wasn't as free as Farmer believed, however, as Baines watched at least two of the dark green

Japanese aircraft burst into flames either from *Victorious*' guns or those of her screen.

The rising roar of an aircraft engine was his only warning to get himself down on the deck. Several of the British officers turned to look at him just before their world was shaken. Baines did not know where the weapon impacted. All he knew was the familiar, high-pitched whine of fragments made his bladder nearly release. The feeling intensified as he heard the screams of men hit by fragments, followed by two more hits that shook the carrier. In a matter of thirty seconds, three more near misses shook the vessel before, yet again, another weapon struck the carrier.

Four hits at least, Baines thought. *Oh sweet Jesus, she's done for.* The *Victorious'* Tannoy began to call for damage control parties to the flight deck and aft hangar deck. Baines regained his feet, looking around the flag bridge to see a gaping hole in the port bulkhead about the size of a man's torso. Smoke was starting to waft up from the hit, the wind of *Victorious'* passage blowing it away from where Baines stood.

Hit in the island, he thought dimly.

"Goddammit! We need to avoid those damn torpedo bombers!" Cunningham shouted. Baines noticed the man's uniform was covered in blood.

Clearly not his own blood, as a man with that much bleeding on his chest would be lying on the deck rather than shouting invective.

There was the sound of another closing aircraft followed immediately by a burst of automatic weapons fire as *Victorious* began to heel over. Baines' eye registered the green-painted torpedo bomber passing from starboard to port, rear gunner blazing away, before his brain could quite process it. The torpedo bomber got roughly two hundred yards off the carrier's side before a wing was sheered off by a pom-pom.

Serves you right, you bastard, Baines thought, clenching his fists. *No one flies over a damn carrier's deck.*

He rushed to look over the flight deck, expecting to look down into a volcano of damage. Instead, while it was clear that the *Victorious* had suffered severe hits, the damage was surprisingly not as horrible as he had thought from the quick succession of hits. A burning aircraft engine and partial, burning dark green fuselage told him some Japanese pilot had not pulled out of his dive.

"I don't think we're bloody going to dodge all of them!" someone shouted. The cry made Baines look out the *Victorious'* side. He saw six tracks, all heading towards the carrier's side even as she was accelerating and heeled over to turn into them. Almost as a precursor of what was about to come, he saw the *Eagle* hit on her starboard side by two torpedoes in quick succession.

Well shit, Baines thought, having a flashback to seeing the U.S.S. *Lexington* in *extremis* right before his own *Saratoga* was hit off Hawaii. Then the *Victorious* was suddenly whipping in seemingly three directions at once. Barnes was knocked off his feet, falling backward into the flag bridge compartment and rolling across the deck. *Victorious'* lights flickered as Baines tried to take a breath, certain the impact with the unforgiving steel had probably cracked some of his ribs. He had barely gotten his wind back when the second Japanese torpedo struck, bouncing him off the deck with the *thunk* of his steel helmet. For a moment Baines lay senseless, the shouts of men around him, gunfire, and alarms all fading into a distant din.

"Lieutenant Commander Baines!" someone was shouting. "Baines! Are you all right?"

"Yes," Baines struggled to speak on his second try. "I'm fine, see to someone else."

He rolled to his knees, the throbbing in his head intensifying as he shifted.

Christ almighty, why do I keep ending up on carriers under attack? Baines asked himself, checking for bumps and bruises. His ankle throbbed a bit, but he was relieved to feel no protruding bones or other signs indicating it was broken. Glancing around the compartment, he saw that at least three members of Vice Admiral Cunningham's staff were down, severely injured.

The sick bay is going to be kinda busy, he thought.

The din of guns began to recede, finally ceasing with a few final shots from the 4.5-inch heavy guns lining *Victorious'* flight deck. Taking a couple of moments to gather himself, Baines staggered to his feet. Weaving like a battered boxer, he went towards the starboard exit, stepped out onto the ladder, and looked down *Victorious'* side. What he saw concerned him, as the carrier was streaming oil, ablaze, and already starting to list and slow.

Judging from the vibration, we've got damage in propulsion of some sort, Baines thought. The carrier was almost certainly headed for the yard for a very long time if she did not sink outright. Ominously, dense, grayish smoke began to pour from the aft lift before his very eyes.

Hope that fancy flight deck of theirs comes with excellent fire extinguishers, Baines thought, gripping the railing. *That looks like a combination of oil and aviation fuel.*

"Sir, Captain Mackintosh wishes to inform you that it may be time to consider shifting your flag," Cunningham's chief of staff, Commander Willis, called from the compartment's rear.

"Tell him to bloody well save this ship and I won't have to worry about shifting my flag," Cunningham retorted as he continued to stare through his glasses at something across the formation. Limping, Baines headed to see what the senior British officer was watching so intently. As the admiral came further out onto the flag bridge platform, Baines saw the decapitated body of Cunningham's secretary.

That's...that's a helluva mess, Baines thought, stomach churning at the blood pooed under the flag secretary's corpse and sprayed all over the surrounding area.

"Stop gawking, Baines, and tell me what you see over there on *Eagle*," Cunningham snapped. "Your damn aviator eyes are better than these old ones."

Baines waited for Cunningham to realize his error in using the plural. Seeing the British admiral was clearly *not* going to comprehend his mistake regarding Baines' vision, the American brought up his own binoculars.

Jesus, she's hard hit, Baines thought, wincing. *Even worse than we are.* As he watched, several explosions occurred on the aft end of the *Eagle*'s flight deck, seemingly from ready ammunition for the stern mounted 6-inch guns.

Not so sure there's ever a good reason to keep cruiser guns on a carrier, Baines thought. *But that's certainly an argument firmly against.*

The deck shifted a bit under his feet as he brought his binoculars down.

"It looks as if she has quite a bit of damage to her stern, with secondary explosions," Baines said, gesturing towards the burning, older carrier. There was a rumble from the *Victorious*' own stern, and Baines looked aft to see a gout of flames erupt from the aft lift.

"It would appear that we have some problems of our own," Cunningham stated, his mouth twisting in a grimace. He looked past Baines as there was movement inside the flag bridge. A few moments later, Lieutenant Commander Farmer and Commander Willis, Cunningham's chief of staff, both made their way out onto the flag bridge's open platform.

"What's the damage to her, Commander Willis?" Cunningham asked, gesturing aft.

"The fuel lines weren't fully empty when we got hit," Willis replied. "That's most of the fire. Thankfully the cofferdams and voids worked as intended, or we'd be abandoning her from one of the torpedo hits. As is, there is aviation fuel leaking into some of the lower spaces."

Cunningham nodded at Willis' report. Baines looked at both men, confused as Willis continued his report.

"The other torpedo struck in propulsion and breached Fireroom No. 1," Willis continued. "Captain Mackintosh brought her to a stop, so the damage wasn't made worse. For now, our top speed is probably eighteen knots."

Dammit, that's not fast enough to launch anything, Baines thought, glancing briefly up towards the national ensign. *Not even those light **Seafires** of theirs.*

"Looks like the *Emerald* is done for," someone said from

behind Baines. He turned to look at the light cruiser and his stomach sank.

The dive bombers made a mess of her, Baines thought. The *Emerald* was burning furiously from amidships, the bridge was visibly blown to pieces, and everything aft of 'Y' turret was a wreck. One of the screening destroyers was making their way toward the *Emerald*'s port side, but Baines was not sure the smaller vessel would make it.

"Sir, I can go below and get a better report from damage control," Farmer stated, gesturing towards the fire. "I wouldn't want to bother Captain Mackintosh."

Cunningham waved at the man to go, also studying the surviving vessels in his formation.

"We'll have to shift to *Prince of Wales* after all," Cunningham said finally. "We'll need one of the destroyers to come alongside to get it done."

"Yes sir," one of the staff stated. Before that man could turn, another was already heading to get the signal made.

I'll say this for Vice Admiral Cunningham, Baines thought, *his staff is efficient as hell*.

"What's the status of *Ark Royal* and *Illustrious*?" Cunningham asked.

"The *Ark Royal* reports she's recovering the CAP, while *Illustrious* is flying off all of her daylight fighters."

"Signal both of them to start heading south, back towards the Maldives," Cunningham said.

"Sir?" Commander Willis asked.

"Clearly the bloody Japanese are closer than we think!" Cunningham snapped. "*Eagle* is done for, *Victorious* is damaged."

The admiral turned his baleful gaze on Baines.

"How many carriers do you figure that was, Baines?!" the man snapped. "More or less than when you got hit at Hawaii."

"At least three decks," Baines replied grimly. "Possible they split their force four and two with the others up at Ceylon."

"Or it's possible that the damn crabs were wrong about

what carriers they saw last night," Cunningham snapped, starting to step towards Baines before having to catch himself against *Victorious*' increasing list. "Either way, it'd be rather nice if there were four American vessels close enough to catch them when those damn aircraft were landing, wouldn't it?"

Well if your damn countrymen weren't playing footsie with the Nazis, we wouldn't have felt it necessary to go finish off those two escort carriers, Baines thought, keeping his face expressionless. He was saved from a potential international incident by an urgent report from one of the staff officers.

"Sir! Captain Mackintosh requests you state your intentions on transferring flag."

Cunningham fixed Baines with one more angry look, then turned to the officer.

"Tell bloody Captain Mackintosh the staff is working on it, and we'll be transferring as quickly as possible," Cunningham replied, his voice cold but level.

Baines realized with a start that *Victorious* had come to a stop. Looking at his watch, he took a shocked breath.

Twenty minutes since we got the first radar contact, he thought, looking up as a solitary *Seafire* passed overhead, *ten minutes tops since we've been hit.*

There was a crash as a navigator's sextant slid off the map behind him. Several other objects began sliding as *Victorious* continued a seemingly inexorable list.

Two torpedoes shouldn't have done that much damage… wait, that's right, the Japanese were believed to have Torpex, or something like it, now, Baines recalled, looking around the compartment for somewhere to be out of the way.

Torpedo explosive, or "Torpex" for short, had been under development by the Admiralty when the Germans had won the Second Battle of Britain. Based on the extensive damage inflicted by the IJN at the Battle of Hawaii, the USN's Office of Naval Intelligence (ONI) had assumed the Germans and Japanese had developed near copies of the formula.

Judging from the fact she's gotta be listing close to ten degrees already, Baines thought as he picked out a nearby stanchion to move to, *I'd say our Japanese friends have definitely improved the formula.*

"I don't mean to help Captain Mackintosh be about his business," Cunningham stated, looking pointedly at Commander Willis, "but shouldn't we be counterflooding?"

"Sir, there was some trouble with the counterflooding valves due to the shock damage," one of the talkers reported. "They've figured out a workaround, but it will take time."

Baines spared another look aft where the fire continued to burn.

I'd be more concerned about that blaze, he thought, pursing his lips. *That's gotta be making things somewhat hot down below.*

Another destroyer, one of the larger "leaders," began nudging up towards the stern play hoses on the *Victorious*. The water hitting the flight deck began to visibly steam, evidence of just how hot the fire burned in the carrier's upper hangar deck.

"Sir, the *Jervis* is coming to pick us up," Commander Willis said as he slammed down a sound-powered phone behind Baines.

Cunningham pointed to the destroyer aiding in putting out the fire on the *Victorious*' stern.

"I think the *Jervis* is quite busy trying to keep this vessel from going sky high," Cunningham observed drily. "Pass command to Vice Admiral Syfret, order *Prince of Wales* to join the *Ark Royal* and *Illustrious*. She's doing no good for us here."

Commander Willis briefly appeared to want to argue with Cunningham but thought better of it.

Vice Admiral Cunningham has a point, Baines thought. *If she stays, all the Prince of Wales will achieve is likely getting herself torpedoed without fighter cover.* **Victorious** *isn't certainly done for, but the next Japanese strike will finish us unless that storm front gets closer, faster.*

The dark, ominous clouds from which the Japanese had come were indeed starting to get closer. Having seen a couple of hurricanes and many gales in his service, Baines had concerns about the approaching storm.

At the very least that's a gale, Baines thought, running a hand through his hair. *I wouldn't be surprised to find out it's a tropical storm.*

"Sir, we should probably get you below to sick bay," another rating, this one different than the one who had handed him the crutches, stated. Looking around the flag bridge and noting that Cunningham's staff was starting to grab essential papers, Baines nodded.

"Lead the way, I can follow along," Baines replied, letting go of the stanchion and balancing on one leg. The rating gave him a dubious look but led the way out of the compartment. As he hopped towards the ladder down towards the bridge, Baines noticed that the *Victorious*' list was starting to decrease. Muttering a prayer of thanks to damage control officers everywhere, he got Willis' attention.

"I'm heading to sick bay," he called across the compartment, realizing that everything seemed muffled as he talked. The British officer nodded, then looked towards where Vice Admiral Cunningham looked over the force. The admiral nodded, then quickly wrote something down on a notepad.

I imagine those are hasty orders, Baines thought, wincing as he began moving across the compartment.

Seeing that his senior was otherwise occupied, Willis made his way over to where Baines stood.

"We cannot wait for you," the commander said, then gestured towards the destroyer aft. "We have to get Vice Admiral Cunningham to somewhere he can command this force."

"I understand," Baines replied grimly. "I don't think I'm exactly someone he wants to talk to for the foreseeable future anyway."

Willis pursed his lips at that.

"Fair or not, he has reason to be upset," the British officer responded. "You've done your duty as well as you could given your orders."

Baines nodded, his own expression flat.

"I'm sorry Admiral King was an idiot," Baines replied. "Vice Admiral Cunningham is right. We'd be able to catch them in one hell of a vise right about now if Vice Admiral Fletcher was in range."

"There's always tomorrow," Willis replied. "That strike sure as hell did not get away without losses."

"There she goes!" a rating shouted, pointing from where he stood near a porthole.

Willis looked pained as he turned to look out at the force. Baines followed the man's gaze. The *Emerald*, severely battered, had finally succumbed to her damage. The cruiser's bow was rising, pointing accusingly into the sky from where her assailants had come.

"I've got to go," Willis said brusquely, visibly angry.

You know, I'd hate to end on these terms, Baines thought. Impulsively, he shot his hand out towards Willis. The Royal Navy officer paused for a moment, then regained his bearing.

"Good luck, Lieutenant Commander Baines," Willis said, meeting Baines' gaze.

"Same to you, Commander Willis," Baines replied.

With a final nod, the chief of staff turned back and strode to where Vice Admiral Cunningham stood. Baines continued hobbling towards the ladder leading down to the *Victorious*' sick bay.

H.M.C.S. Ark Royal
1330 Local

"Those bloody new kites were just as bad as we expected," Marshall spat angrily, then nearly screamed as the corpsman continued stitching his arm up.

I can only hope that I am so coherent after smashing my damaged fighter into the flight deck, Venkata thought, hands still in his pockets to hide their shaking. *Because that was the most intense five minutes of my life.*

"What did you think, Venkata?" Marshall asked, starting to gesture with his right arm and immediately paying for it.

"Sir, I don't mean to be rude, but we're going to have to take you down to sick bay and strap you down if you keep this up," the corpsman stated drily. "I know it's difficult for you pilots to talk without your hands, but unless you want to lose the arm, *let me work.*"

Venkata thanked luck, God, or his ancestors for the pause. The twelve pilots gathered around Marshall at the front of the hangar deck were in varied states of dishevelment. Like Marshall and Venkata, three stood with their uniforms soaked in sweat. *Ark Royal*'s scrambled fighters had arrived in time to try and avenge *Victorious*, but little else. Even that was beyond Marshall and Venkata's grasp, as they had swiftly run into five Japanese fighters.

"I'm thinking that it would be best if we did not try a head on run with any of them in the future," Venkata said quietly.

Now why did you say that, Venkata? he thought angrily, wanting to just melt through the deck beneath him. Looking up at him in initial surprise, Marshall's mouth then split into a wide grin.

"Cheeky bastard," the squadron leader said, then turned to the rest of the group. "What Flight Lieutenant Singh is *not* mentioning is that while *I* came off not so well in my head on run, *he* shot down the bastard's wingman. Then got another one of them with a deflection shot."

I'm still not so sure about that second one, Singh thought, shrugging.

"Hope it doesn't come to that for some of us," one of the *Martlet* pilots stated, his face pale. "The Yanks built these birds tough, but..."

The man was cut off by a rating nearly falling down the ladder and onto the upper hangar deck. The sailor hit like a bag of potatoes, shouting expletives as he rolled around on the deck.

"Bloody hell," Marshall said, then turned to the corpsman. "Go see to that idiot, we can finish this in a second."

As if spurred by Marshall's comment, the man staggered to his feet. Venkata noticed that he heard several other sailors running at the far end of the hangar deck and distant shouting.

"The bloody Tannoy's out!" the sailor shouted. "Pilots man your planes! Man your bloody planes!"

Before Marshall could respond, the aforementioned loudspeaker gave a loud screech, a stretch of static, and several clicks.

"Is the damn thing working now, you idiot?!" the familiar voice of *Ark Royal*'s XO filled the hangar. Apparently realizing he was now transmitting, the carrier's second-in-command began the required litany informing the ship's company of imminent air attack.

What?! Venkata thought, looking back toward where the *Spitfire* he'd been flying that morning waited to be refueled. *What planes?!*

Thinking quickly and without further conversation, he turned and sprinted for the ladder up to the deck.

First pilot to the bird gets to take off, he thought. *I'm not sitting on this damn ammunition and fuel dump if I can help it.*

The air from the flight deck was a welcome relief from the sweltering hotbox down below. Near the stern, an empty *Spitfire* was being wheeled towards launch position, the crew chief looking expectantly for a pilot. Venkata, after a quick check to make sure there were no spinning propellers, headed directly for the Supermarine.

"Sir, where's..." the petty officer started to inquire before Venkata cut him off.

"Get it ready, we've got to scramble!" he shouted. "The damn Japanese are inbound."

Nodding once, the crew chief shouted at the crew to preflight the fighter. Looking back down the flight deck,

Venkata saw the remaining *Seafire* pilots making their way down the deck. Several of the men walked noticeably slower than the others.

Some of these pilots are clearly 'fought out,' he thought. *I don't care what that idiot Vice Admiral Cunningham thinks, there needs to be a rest plan for these pilots. Otherwise he'll have carriers without anyone to fly the birds.*

"You're ready to go, sir!" the crew chief said. "Good luck!"

"Thank you!" Venkata replied. The petty officer slid off his wing just as the first *Seafire* in line began rolling down the *Ark Royal*'s flight deck.

Oh shit, he thought. *I don't even know what flight position I'm in.* A quick count made his heart rise in his throat. His *Seafire* was in the third position, meaning that he was a section leader.

Well, needs must and all that.

Venkata, you are a bloody idiot, and you're about to get yourself killed.

It had been ten minutes since he'd finally gotten off *Ark Royal*'s deck. Now, as he listened to the guidance from the carrier's fighter direction officer (FDO), it was sinking in just how outnumbered the Royal Navy's combat air patrol was.

How did the Japanese get off two strikes so fast? he wondered. *I'm no carrier expert, but this is insanity!*

"Roger Shilling Base, understand that Griffin and Manticore flights are to take the torpedo bombers down low, Archer and Yeoman flights bandits at angels ten," Lieutenant Gratham replied. As the ranking officer airborne, he'd assumed command of the ragtag CAP as Archer leader. *Ark Royal*'s FDO, to his credit, had quickly ascertained that there were more *Martlet* and *Sea Hurricanes* than *Seafires* airborne.

*Guess we'll see if **Illustrious**' air wing actually gets into the fight*, Venkata thought bitterly. *Not exactly helpful to have blokes flying around as night fighters when your enemy apparently isn't a bunch of Narrah.* Although Venkata was well aware that the

Japanese had several night bomber squadrons, he'd only heard of them operating from land bases, not carriers.

"Shilling Base, Shilling Base, this is Nighthawk Leader," another voice sounded across the radio network. "I have businessmen ready to do trade, with my good friends Kestrel Flight available in roughly one zero minutes."

If on cue, Venkata thought. He listened as the FDO aboard *Ark Royal* gave hurried instructions to the *Illustrious*' squadron of *Gannet*s.

Not sure I'd be weighting my effort so heavily towards the torpedo bombers, mate, Venkata mused. He turned to look off his port forward at the pall of smoke that had the *Victorious* at its base.

*Then again, the fact **Victorious** is still immobile might indicate he's onto something*, Venkata thought. He also noticed that the *Ark Royal*'s FDO was not allocating any additional fighters to cover the fleet's flagship or the equally damaged *Eagle*.

"Tallyho! Tallyho! Many bandits, eleven o'clock low!"

Jesus, how many aircraft do the Japanese have? Venkata thought, seeing the distant dots as they were finally visible against the darkened storm front behind them. Even as he watched, several of the dots began to break off and climb towards them as the *Seafires* turned to meet them.

"Ignore the fighters! Get after those dive bombers!" Gratham barked.

Checking for his wingman, Venkata put his *Seafire* into a slight climb and pushed the throttle through to emergency war power. The fighter began to shake from the extra strain, but he watched as the maneuver had the desired effect of getting him additional altitude without losing much airspeed. Archer Four was right behind him as the gaggle of RN fighters passed over their opposite Japanese numbers.

Going to only get one lick before that lot comes in back behind us, Venkata thought grimly. Quickly scanning the approaching Japanese force, he noticed it was beginning to split apart.

*Well, small mercy that they're going to send some blokes to finish off the **Victorious** and **Eagle***, Venkata thought. *Although now* *that this is a tail chase, that's no good.* The Japanese bombers, even heavily laden, were quite fast for their types. *Ark Royal*'s FDO had done them a solid by placing them high and abeam the attacking aircraft, but only on the assumption the entire strike would be coming for the two remaining untouched carriers, not splitting.

***Victorious** will have to see to herself,* Venkata thought, breaking off his turn to arc after a trio of Japanese bombers.

"Archer Four, take the starboard one," he gritted out, his vision shrinking as he pulled a tight turn. Out of the corner of his eye, he could see three Japanese fighters coming in towards him.

You bastards shouldn't be able to get the angle…

The green dive bomber swelled in his gunsight. Tracers arced towards him from the tail gunner, the initial burst far wide. Venkata didn't give the man a chance to correct his aim, squeezing the firing button for a short burst. His own fire was initially wide, but then the streams of tracer from his twin 20-mm cannon and their matching .50-caliber machine guns sawed into the bomber's fuselage. Venkata had just let up on the trigger when one of the last rounds detonated his target's payload in a reddish-black flash.

Bloody hell! Venkata thought as something that looked suspiciously like an engine hurtled past his canopy. The *Seafire* shuddered from other debris impacts, but Venkata barely had time to glance over his gauges before a trio of angry *Shiden* fighters was upon him. He skidded the *Seafire* to the left as the Japanese leader fired at him, the four 20mm rounds going beneath his nose. The two Japanese wingmen hurtled by without firing, their noses rising as they began pulling up.

No, I don't think I'll kill myself today, Venkata thought, gaining separation from the trio of *Shiden*. Unfortunately, his pell-mell run from that trio brought him closer to *another* trio that had been chasing a *Gannet*. Venkata turned into the second attacking group, only to nearly have his canopy blown off by the now reversed leader of the second group.

"Archer Four, where are you?" he asked crossly, then realized his voice was just another in a cacophony of men fighting for their lives. Pulling back on the stick, he put the *Seafire* into a tight turn...and nearly collided with another *Shiden*. Startled, the Japanese pilot pulled up and away from Venkata, only to be blotted from the sky by a diving *Sea Hurricane*. Venkata lost track of that fighter as the original Japanese leader slid into view in his rearview mirror from having rolled across Venkata's turn.

*Bloody hell...*Venkata thought, seeing the hostile fighter's wings start to flash. The *Seafire* shuddered from several hits somewhere aft in the fuselage, then the *Shiden* was falling away as it stalled. Whipping his head around, Venkata saw a *Shiden* arcing down in flames nearby, then a sky seemingly empty other than the falling *Shiden* off to port. He rolled the *Seafire* in that direction, arcing down after the recovering Japanese fighter.

"Not today, mate," Venkata said grimly, putting his pipper just forward of the enemy fighter's nose and firing. While it did not burn as readily as a *Zero*, the *Shiden* still made a satisfying winged bonfire as his cannon and machine guns pierced its fuel tanks.

Hope the gun camera got that, Venkata thought, immediately putting his fighter into a tight, cautionary turn. In the distance, he could see the storm of anti-aircraft fire over the *Ark Royal* and *Illustrious* task force. Seeing no nearby enemy, he immediately set out toward the ongoing attack.

I won't get there in time, he thought. *Bloody well will kill some of those bastards as they leave though*.

Unfortunately for the Royal Navy the storm of anti-aircraft fire, while dramatic, was not as effective as its leaders would have hoped.

Commander Mitsuo Fuchida, having foregone a torpedo for his own *Tenzan* in lieu of extra fuel, had turned back to coordinate the second strike. As was his nature, *Akagi*'s CAG had once again gotten greedy with the *Kido Butai*'s strike abilities. Fuchida's orders had been explicit, with Vice Admiral Tamon Yamaguchi directing that he concentrate on crippling as many ships as possible rather than sinking only a few. It was a stance that Fuchida vehemently disagreed with, which was why he split the second strike almost in half to ensure *Victorious'* and *Eagle*'s destruction.

Unfortunately for the dive and torpedo bombers assigned to the second strike, this meant that the *Kido Butai*'s fighters were divided between two prongs of attack. British FDOs on the *Ark Royal* and, for the handful of fighters over the crippled carriers, the heavy cruiser *Berwick*, maximized their limited resources. Although not nearly enough to *stop* the *Kido Butai*'s assault, the desperate British fighters did manage to sow sufficient chaos that twelve of the *Tenzan* torpedo bombers went after the venerable *Malaya* and *Warspite* rather than concentrating on the *Ark Royal* and *Illustrious*.

In the case of the *Warspite*, the vessel's famous luck held once again as all six of her assailants missed. Adding insult to injury, two *Tenzan* paid the ultimate price for having the temerity to attack their elder. The remaining four would return to their carriers in various degrees of damage and breathless reports of having attacked a well-handled *King George V* battleship in the company of an older *Queen Elizabeth*-class vessel. They would also erroneously claim two hits on the *Warspite*, making yet another group of opponents that believed they had hit the "Grand Old Lady."

Unfortunately for the "older" *Malaya*, she had not undergone as thorough a modification as her sister between the world wars. Moreover, her crew was not nearly as experienced as *Warspite*'s, having spent most of the early part of the war escorting merchant convoys. For these reasons, all six *Tenzan* attacking the battleship not only survived to drop their torpedoes but did so in a textbook hammer and anvil attack. Turning to port to avoid one *chutai*, *Malaya* doomed herself to three hits from starboard.

Arguably the *Queen Elizabeth*-class, when built, had enjoyed the Royal Navy's best underwater protection of the First World War. Alas for Vice Admiral Syfret, his staff, and the battleship's crew, torpedo technology had evolved in the twenty-seven years since *Malaya*'s commissioning. Thus the trio of hits, grouped tightly together, in effect opened the *Malaya*'s starboard side to the Indian Ocean from her amidships almost to her entire stern. Gushing oil, steam, and listing rapidly, the flagship began rapidly slowing and rolling onto her beam ends.

The elderly battleship's inadvertent destruction was not wholly useless. Rather than facing almost two dozen torpedo bombers in addition to twenty dive bombers, the *Illustrious* and *Ark Royal* were set upon by only six torpedo bombers. Unfortunately for *Ark Royal*, the *Illustrious* once again successfully found a rain squall where her slower compatriot was caught barely a half mile short. Balancing this out, however, the *Ark Royal* was left with a far heavier screen as the cruisers *Danae* and *Despatch* hove away from *Illustrious* prior to entering the squall.

Having learned lessons from their unsuccessful defense of the *Victorious*, the *Prince of Wales*' crew managed to stay in much closer escort to their charge this time. Complemented by the two light cruisers' meager anti-aircraft fire and the worsening weather, the anti-aircraft defense was *just* enough to keep the *Ark Royal* from suffering fatal damage. Three 1,000-lb. bombs pierced the carrier's unarmored flight deck, blasting the carrier's elevator out of the flight deck, wrecking the aft hangar, and killing the ship's surgeon plus a repair party. Hardly had the vessel stopped whipsawing from those blasts when two torpedoes hit her, one on each side amidships and aft. In a stroke, the carrier's power was knocked out, her belowdecks rendered dark except where her fires illuminated passageways. Grimly, her crew set about trying to shore up bulkheads and eliminate blazes even as the carrier's fighters fought the Japanese above.

. . .

Venkata gripped the control yoke with impotent rage as he hurtled past the *Ark Royal*'s outer screen. A few black bursts off to his port side reminded him that it would be foolish to approach the screen any closer, but it was easy to see the carrier was in dire straits.

I'm going to go find someone to kill, he thought. *I mean, she hasn't been my ship for long, but **no one** messes with your airdrome.*

A glint of sunlight off a canopy caught his attention to starboard. Turning, he sighted a trio of Japanese aircraft—one torpedo bomber and two fighters—orbiting. The trio were roughly four miles away and clearly fixated on the spectacle that was the *Ark Royal* beneath them.

As the Yanks say, one pass, haul ass, Venkata thought, turning to get upsun from the Japanese aircraft. Making one last glance to ensure he didn't have his own stalker, he put the *Spitfire* into a shallow dive.

Wait for it...wait for it, he thought, seeing the Japanese bomber swelling in his gunsight. The starboard fighter clearly saw him, pulling up.

Too late, you wank...what the fuck?

The explosion that caused his surprise was so violent it briefly caused him to jerk. Unfortunately it did the same for his target. Venkata screamed in frustration as his burst scored some hits, shattering the canopy and knocking debris off the main fuselage.

Dammit! Dammit! Dammit!

Venkata briefly considered turning around but thought better of it as he continued running away from the two Japanese fighters. As he dived, he took stock of the situation in front of him. There was a roiling, expanding cloud of black smoke where the *Malaya* had been. To the north, another pall of smoke told him nothing good had happened to the *Victorious* task force. With genuine concern, he looked at his fuel gauge.

Where the hell are we all going to land?

H.M.C.S. Illustrious
1635 Local

"I saw him die myself, sir."

The grim pronouncement, in an accent that marked the speaker as an American, was delivered calmly. So much so that Servius was not sure he'd heard what he thought he had while walking into the *Illustrious*' flag bridge. The next sentence, however, confirmed it.

"Vice Admiral Cunningham was standing right in front of me when the explosion happened," the American, a lieutenant commander from the looks of it, continued. The man's uniform was soaked, with a faint smell of bunker oil wafting off him. Servius noted the man's arm was in a sling and he favored one leg standing before Vian.

Hope no one lights a match, Servius thought grimly. *There have been quite enough fires aboard Her Majesty's vessels today.*

Rear Admiral Philip Vian, apparently now the ranking Royal Navy officer in the Indian Ocean, pursed his lips in annoyance at the American's statement. A gaunt, tall man, Vian had built a reputation for being no nonsense from the very beginning of the war.

When you've commanded the Royal Navy's most recent boarding action, Servius mused, *most people tend to assume you'll just slash an arm off with a cutlass. Then there's this Yank...*

"Rear Admiral Vian did not ask for theatrics, Lieutenant Command..." Commander John Flint, Vian's Chief of Staff, began. Before Flint could finish his admonishment, the American cut him off.

"Asshole, if I was being *theatrical*, I would have mentioned the fragment of your damned flight deck sliced the side of his head open like it was a cantaloupe," the American seethed, accent thick with his anger. "If you've wondered whether your superiors actually have brains in their heads, I can now testify to the affirmative."

Jesus, Servius thought, seeing looks of shock and disgust

that likely mirror his own. *That's our commander you're talking about, you bloody bell end.*

"Gentlemen, that's enough," Vian said, his voice calm but firm. "Thank you, Lieutenant Commander Baines. Regrettably, we don't have a new uniform for you. However, I'm sure Commander Flint can find a Royal Navy uniform in your size."

Baines looked around the bridge like a caged animal, the veins still throbbing in his neck.

Are we about to have to sedate the man? Servius thought. After a moment, Baines seemed to regain his composure, a slight flush coming to his face.

"I'm sorry, sir," he said. "It's been...there's been a lot this morning."

Vian nodded sympathetically.

"We'll have the *Illustrious*' flight surgeon give you something so you can rest," Vian said, locking eyes with Flint. The chief of staff nodded.

"Right this way, Lieutenant Commander," Flint said stiffly. Baines limped after the man, wincing with every step as he walked past Servius. After watching them depart, Servius turned back towards Vian. The flag officer's expression was bleak as he studied Servius.

"So, it would appear that a force which began this morning believing we would be finding combat with our Japanese counterparts on the 'morrow has learned the perils of trusting allies and believing intelligence reports," Vian noted.

A bit harsh on the Americans, Servius thought. *But I didn't just have command land on me like a ton of bricks.*

"As I have no desire to have our partners possibly commenting on whether my skull contains wood or brains," Vian continued, "I would like to know if you can torpedo carriers as well as submarines."

Servius swallowed as he felt the blood run from his face.

"Yes, sir," he said after a moment. "But I have to admit, it would seem the odds are a bit stiff for eight *Tarpon*s. We would almost certainly need an escort."

Vian laughed.

"Well, at least I know that you torpedo lads didn't leave your balls in your *Swordfish*," Vian said.

Oh, thank the gods, Servius thought, smiling nervously. *I thought for certain he was going to send us out to earn a posthumous Victoria Cross, accomplishing less than the Light Brigade.*

"In any case, an escort would be out of the question," Vian replied. "I have every fighter that can fly over the *Ark Royal*. Not that they'll be able to stop the Japanese if they really try to finish her off. But I'm hoping whoever's on the other side will be satiated with what he's accomplished today and turn his eyes to wherever the damn Yanks are."

"That does seem to be the million pound question, doesn't it?" Servius snapped. He stopped and took a moment to regain his composure as Vian regarded him. "Sorry sir."

"Oh no, by all means, I am quite cross with them also," Vian said. "We've lost a lot of good men today, and I'd personally like to know where in the hell Fletcher is."

We assume some misfortune hasn't befallen him, Servius thought. That possibility sent a positive chill down his spine, and he forced the thought from his head. Looking at the map in the center of *Illustrious*' flag bridge, he narrowed his eyes.

"Sir, how accurate is this plot?" he asked, pointing.

Vian looked over at the duty officer, a young lieutenant.

"The report is just over an hour old, sir," the young man replied. "A *Sunderland* made it. We have not heard from it since."

No, I imagine not, Servius thought. *Plane that slow sights four, possibly five, fleet carriers it's not going to live long. Especially as the Japanese allegedly have radar now.*

Servius did some quick mental calculations.

"The Japanese have to be heading away from us, sir," he replied. "Or else they can hit us from a much longer range than either our or the Americans' intelligence believes."

Vian snorted at that.

"I mean, wouldn't be the first thing that people got wrong today, would it?" the senior officer asked.

Servius pursed his lips, working geometry in his head.

"Sir, what are your intentions?" he asked. Vian looked at him quizzically.

Should probably explain the whole sentence, you fool!

"If you wish to pursue the enemy, I have an idea," Servius continued. Vian's look went from quizzical to clearly wondering if Servius was mad.

"Sir, I assure you, I have no intention of getting mentioned in despatches followed by the Queen giving my family a wonderful medal named for one of her predecessors," Servius said.

"It's not your person I'm worried about," Vian commented grimly. "We seem to be losing admirals at a stunning rate in this war, and I'd rather not have my name adorn a future battleship."

"Sir, this carrier has a unique capability," Servius continued. "One our opponents cannot match. I believe we should take advantage of this during the hours of darkness."

"So you're thinking a night torpedo strike after all?" Vian asked.

"No sir," Servius said quickly. "During our operations off of British Columbia with the Americans, we devised a modification for our *Tarpons*. We can add a fuel tank in place of the torpedo. All of my birds have the requisite plumbing for it. Alas, No. 885 Squadron's *Tarpon*s do not."

Vian nodded, signaling Servius to continue.

"If we harass the Japanese throughout the night, they'll likely come back after us," Servius said. "Except we won't be where they think we'll be because, with that fuel tank, the *Tarpon* has an additional 150 miles of range."

Actually, an extra two hundred, but I don't want to possibly condemn people to ditching *at night because we erased their margin,* Servius thought.

"Go on," Vian said.

"We can even make matters worse by occasionally dropping flares and feinting towards the enemy," Servius continued. "Anything to harass him and keep him awake."

"To what end, though?" Vian inquired. "Although you weren't here when the staff briefed it, *Ark Royal* is a cripple until she reaches a repair ship or a drydock. Neither of which, I might add, we have at the Maldives."

It is annoying, at times, dealing with non-aviators, Servius thought. He chewed the inside of his cheek, pondering how to proceed tactfully.

"Out with it," Vian said, his tone belying the shortness of his words. "We have no time to stand on niceties, so pretend I'm the village idiot."

Servius felt a surge of deep respect for Vian.

It takes a confident man to show he doesn't know everything, he thought.

"Sir, if we make the Japanese come south to finish us off, that buys Ceylon time," Servius said. "It will cost them aircraft, it will cost them fuel and, if we time it right, we will greatly minimize the risk to ourselves even with their apparent greater range."

Vian looked at Servius, his face expressionless.

I guess I need to sweeten the pot.

"It also increases the chance that Fletcher will catch them unawares."

Vian pursed his lips at that.

"I think two admirals dying due to counting on the Americans is enough," Vian muttered waspishly. "But your argument concerning Ceylon is sound."

Vian looked out of the *Illustrious*' island, back to the north.

"Vice Admiral Cunningham used to always go on about the Royal Navy's tradition," he continued. "When he gave his fighting instructions for this operation, he reminded all of us that the Royal Navy could build capital ships in four to five years. We could not, should we lose our tradition and reason for being, restore the work of centuries."

Servius nodded at the comment.

"I do hope our American allies eventually decide to stop galivanting around after stray Italians," Vian said. "Indeed, it would seem they should have a higher interest in smashing some Japanese about than chasing a couple of Italian battleships."

Servius shrugged.

"I do not pretend to understand their navy, sir," Servius stated. "I just know they make fine aircraft."

"Yes, yes they do," Vian nodded, gesturing down toward the *Illustrious*' crowded flight deck. "The only problem is that we have so many of them aboard now. I'll order *Unicorn* to close with us. She was delivering additional fighters to the Maldives."

Servius fought to keep his face neutral.

"Sir, the *Unicorn* is a depot ship," he stated. "If you fight her like a carrier, we will lose her."

"If I don't bring her forward, we will lose this vessel and *Ark Royal*," Vian said. "We simply cannot cycle fighters fast enough through a single flight deck to maintain a strong CAP."

After yesterday, I'm not sure we can put a strong enough CAP in the air, Servius thought.

As if reading his mind, Vian continued.

"We will run north to carry out your plan. Make sure you have your best pilots in the last aircraft, as they will need to stretch their fuel as much as possible."

Servius nodded, understanding Vian.

"In an hour, I will send my aide back to Addu Atoll with my plan and to coordinate with Field Marshall Brand, the RAF commander there," Vian continued. Servius looked at him in shock.

"That's a name I have not heard in a long time," Servius replied. "I had heard he took on retirement and departed for New Zealand during The Lull."

Amazing how many Commonwealth officers thought we were being idiots for trusting Himmler and took the opportunity to go home, Servius thought. *Now, they're the bulk of the experienced leaders we have left.*

"Yes, well, hopefully he can bring some of his magic from the First Battle of Britain to what I hope is an engagement in the morning," Vian stated. "Your fellow air officers tell me that *Beaufighters* and some of those American aircraft can reach out this far."

Oh dear, Servius thought. *Crabs having to do overwater navigation at that distance?*

"Sir, might I suggest that we ensure the RAF is provided a *Sunderland* or some other craft to provide help?"

Vian searched Servius' face.

"There are not an abundance of flying boats about," Vian said. "You may recall there are many Japanese submarines in the area."

"Yes, sir," Servius replied. "I can also assure you that you will kill half of those men if you require them to do long-range navigation over the open ocean."

Vian appeared to want to say something, then reconsidered.

"If a man who is contemplating flying several hours in the darkness to harass a superior force tells me something is too fraught with danger, I ought to listen," Vian said. "I'll include directions for the Coastal Command contingent to detail the necessary aircraft. But if we end up with a torpedo in the side of this carrier, I will be quite cross with you."

"Sir, surely you have more faith in your fellow destroyermen than that," Servius blurted. He felt warmth on his face as he considered the insult. To his relief, Vian laughed.

"I suppose you have a point there, don't you?" the admiral replied. "If the escort can't keep an I-boat out of the screen, there's no reason to expect the aircraft to."

Vian glanced at the clock.

"Well then, I suppose you better get to sleep," he said. "I imagine you'll have a long night ahead of you."

Servius nodded at the dismissal.

"Thank you, sir," he said. "Hopefully we'll meet Vice Admiral Cunningham's intent on the morrow."

Plus it's probably time McGee's men get some time flying antisubmarine patrols, Servius thought.

SOWING CHAOS...

Impetuosity and audacity often achieve what ordinary means fail to achieve—**Machiavelli**

H.M.C.S. ILLUSTRIOUS
0200 LOCAL
INDIAN OCEAN, NORTH OF ADDU
10 AUGUST

"Mate...mate...wake up."

The gentle shake accompanying the voice was what actually brought Baines out of his nightmare. For a moment, his mind played terrible, horrible tricks on him, reality and dreamscape merging in the darkened compartment. Then, with a start, he realized that the juxtaposition was due to the *Illustrious'* officer country being almost exactly the twin to *Victorious'* accommodations.

Note to self, Baines thought. *Make sure allies do not make you **sleep** aboard the sister ship to the vessel that was just blown out from under you.*

"Sorry," Baines said to the figure in the darkness.

"It is quite all right," the man replied. "No one here has had a decent night's sleep since September 1939."

Baines chuckled at that comment.

"I'm sorry, I don't remember your name," Baines said, sitting up in his cot.

"Owens," the man replied. "Jeremy Owens, Fleet Air Arm. Late of the carrier *Eagle*."

Oh damn, Baines thought. *Yep, all of us orphans are gathering together today.*

"I'm not surprised you don't remember," Owens continued, yawning. "Pretty sure the Flight Surgeon slipped you a mickey."

Baines shook his head.

"That would explain the nightmares," he replied. "Most people go into a deep sleep when they go under. I'm the poor bastard who ends up having the worst nightmares imaginable."

Screams from down the passageway caused Baines to whip his head around. After a moment, they stopped.

"As you can hear," Owens said drily, "you are not alone on the nightmares part. Probably just the flavor changes, but the terror remains. If my uncle is to be believed, it's until we die."

Baines rubbed his eye, the silence in the compartment awkward.

Suddenly understand why many men involved in the Great War drank themselves into an early grave or had "accidents," Baines thought, standing up.

"Well damn the luck, I'm fully awake, unfortunately," he said. "I guess I'll head up to the flag bridge and see if I can be of any use."

There was a *thump* of an aircraft recovering on the flight deck above. Baines looked at his watch again, then up at the overhead.

"Okay, that's just not right," he muttered, stepping over to the chair where he'd left his uniform. To his surprise, it was clean and pressed.

Damn efficient laundrymen they have on this boat, he thought. *I was certain that I'd be in Royal Navy blue for the next week.*

"They've been doing flights since around twenty

hundred," Owens replied. "I knew she was a night carrier, but it's wholly different being aboard."

"I'd be worried I'd wander into my own propeller," Baines replied, starting to pull on his uniform. "Why are they launching at night? Have the Japanese been chasing us?"

Owens laughed at that.

"No," he said. "I'd actually like our odds better if they were, quite honestly."

You clearly do not know anyone who is in the surface fleet, Baines thought, buttoning his tunic. *Sounds like the **worst** time to face the Japanese is at night.*

Baines had run into one of his classmates while in Australia. Over beers, one Lieutenant Commander Michael Moran had filled him in on the insanity that had been the defense of the Dutch East Indies.

"I certainly wouldn't want to be on a *carrier* during a surface fight," Baines replied emphatically. "Regardless of how well I thought it might go. Sooner be on a destroyer in a hurricane."

*I hope the **Pillsbury** is nice and safe on that regular convoy run he has to American Samoa,* Baines thought. *Woman sticks with you all the way through Annapolis, you shouldn't make her a widow after four kids.*

"At least the water's warm," Owens replied, breaking Baines' reverie. "Once you've had your balls try to go back up into your body, it's a sensation you never want to repeat."

Baines glanced over at the other man in the darkness.

"I was on the *Glorious*," Owens said simply. "Stupid captain was in a hurry to get back to court-martial a bloke. Or at least, that was the rumor I heard when the Germans repatriated me back during The Lull."

"You know, I heard members of Cunningham's staff keep talking about 'The Lull' when I was aboard the *Victorious*," Baines said, looking about for his cover. Owens answered him as he found the hat.

"It's what some of the Commonwealth folks started calling the time period after Churchill's cabinet forced him to sign that ceasefire with Himmler," Owens replied. "Guess we've all been in Australia long enough it's started to stick."

"Why The Lull?" Baines asked, searching for his shoes.

"You can turn a light on, mate," Owens replied. "I can get back to sleep fairly easy, you won't keep me up."

"Thank you," Baines said, then snapped on the deskside lamp. Looking down, he saw a pair of black shoes where his brown ones had previously been.

"To answer your question, calling it 'Dance of the Village Idiots' or 'The Great Hoodwink' would probably seem rather rude," Owens answered, shifting in his bunk. "You look like you're biting down on a lemon, mate. Shoes the wrong size?"

"No, actually, they're not," Baines replied, chuckling. "It's just that most naval aviators would not be caught dead wearing black shoes."

Owens raised an eyebrow.

"Is this a strange Yank custom I haven't been made aware of?" Owens asked, clearly perplexed.

"I'll explain it some other time," Baines replied with a smile. "Pretty sure you need to get some rest, and I should probably get up to the flag bridge."

"Bold of you to assume we're both going to survive tomorrow," Owens stated, a smirk belying his words.

"After being one of only two pilots to survive from my squadron when *Saratoga*'s magazine went up back in March, then having Vice Admiral Cunningham and his chief of staff cut down in front of me," Baines began, "I'm starting to think I'm cursed to survive this war."

"Well, glad to know I'm roommates with a fellow 'Jonah,'" Owens said, extending his hand. "There, it's sorted. You can tell me all about your shoe aversion when we're both hanging onto one of the Carley Floats in a few hours."

Baines took the hand.

"I can only hope that this vessel has a cook who can make fried chicken for our picnic," he replied, shaking firmly. "Hopefully Vice Admiral Fletcher shows up to ruin our plans."

Bies One
0310 Local
Point Silver, Indian Ocean

"Well, I think we definitely woke up the locals," Lieutenant Barker said, his tone droll.

You know, there is something fundamentally psychotic about us as a people, Servius thought, *that we do our damnedest not to let our stark terror show in times of stress.*

Grunting, Servius gave the *Tarpon* as much starboard rudder as the aircraft could handle without stalling. Streams of tracers arced out towards their low flying bomber, the overwhelming majority of the rounds going far wide. It was the more accurate ones, however, that were causing Servius some consternation. Someone aboard the Japanese destroyer roughly 3,000 yards to their port knew how to apply lead, and Servius felt his stomach drop as the burst went roughly where the *Tarpon* would have been if he'd not evaded.

"Yes, well, fear of getting a torpedo into their side will do that, sir," Petty Officer Daniels chimed in. "Although I must say that concern is vanishingly small compared to the sheer terror involved in counting white tops. White tops one can see despite, of course, it raining sideways."

"How about you both bloody look for those fighters Biers Two thought he saw," Servius snapped, focusing on his instruments lest he put the *Tarpon* into the sea.

"Sir, with all due respect, I couldn't see them even if they are out there," Barker replied. "I don't even know how that destroyer saw us in between these squalls."

"Because we bloody well nearly ran into his mast, that's how," Servius replied, leveling off. He took a deep, shuddering breath as Biers Two once more transmitted their estimated location via Morse code "in the clear."

I hope the damn Americans are able to hear that, he thought, taking his hand off the throttle to open and close his cramping fingers.

"Sir, is that position correct?" Barker asked. Servius could hear the man shifting a map around.

"If you're about to look at that map, bloody well make sure the red lens is on this time," Servius snapped, half turning in his seat.

There was a long pause, followed by a very quiet assent from Barker.

"As for our position, why do you ask?" Servius asked, scanning the skies as Bies One abruptly departed the squall.

"Well, it's just that we're roughly sixty miles south of Bies Three's very first sighting report," Barker said, his tone worried.

Bloody hell, they've come about, Servius thought, a sour feeling growing in the pit of his stomach. *Looks like they mean to finish us off in the morning.*

"Looks like we're going to be stopping at least one more strike for Vice Admiral Fletcher," Servius said, shaking his head in the darkness.

"Hope the Americans tell our widows..." Barker began.

"*Fighter! Six o'clock low!*" Daniels screamed, then immediately began firing his machine gun. The outgoing fire was only a split second ahead of the four streams of tracers that passed just behind the *Tarpon*. Servius dived, turning into a corkscrew as he saw a dark shape hurtle upwards past their fighter.

That bugger nearly got us, Servius thought, focusing on his instruments rather than the rapidly approaching Indian Ocean below. Barker cursed and opened fire, just as there were several impacts at the rear of the *Tarpon*'s fuselage. As the altimeter passed three hundred feet, Servius kicked the rudder to side slip, tracers arcing just past the *Tarpon*.

If you're shooting at me, you're probably not watching where you're going, Servius thought, biting down on his tongue in concentration. *About the only time I'll miss a Stringbag!*

With that last thought, he pulled back on the stick. The

Tarpon's frame groaned with the g-forces, and for a brief moment he was terrified that he had misjudged the torpedo bomber's abilities. Then they were level, engine roaring, thundering along...and a huge splash to their starboard front told Servius he'd guessed right on his opponent's target fixation.

That just might calm them down a bit, he thought, feeling the sweat trickling down his spine.

"Crew, damage report!"

"There's a couple of bloody cannon holes in the fucking radar set, sir," Barker said, his tone angry.

"I can smell fuel, sir," Daniels chimed in. "Not a lot of it, but we leaked something."

Dear Lord, please tell me that wasn't the extra tank, Servius thought, eyes darting to the fuel gauge and back. Taking another glance around, he returned his gaze to the fuel gauges.

Okay, thank God, we don't seem to be losing any at an appreciable rate, he reckoned, then turned his eyes back forward.

"Sir, should we contact Bies Two and tell them we didn't auger in?" Barker asked.

Servius watched as another handful of flares exploded into life on the far side of the Japanese formation.

That's how you know things are incredibly chaotic, Servius thought. *We nearly got separated by twenty miles from Bies Two.*

"Send the code word Odysseus," he ordered, using the code he'd issued for any aircraft forced to return with damage. "Inform him in the code of the day that he's to break off in another ten minutes."

"Aye, aye, sir," Barker said.

"If they've already somehow got one cats eye fighter up," Servius noted, referring to the method of night hunting with only bare vision, "there's probably another one."

The sky behind them once again became alight with searchlights and, in a couple of cases, tracers. The latter converged on a spot at low altitude and, to his horror, Servius saw a ball of fire burst into view.

"Blimey," Daniels breathed, his sentiment speaking for the entire crew.

"Persephone," their headphones crackled with Bies Two's distinctive Cockney accent. "I say again, Persephone."

"*It was an own goal!*" Barker shouted, his joyous lurching slightly shaking the *Tarpon*.

"That should make the odds slightly better tomorrow," Daniels muttered. Servius thought briefly about chastising the man, then thought better of it.

"Bies Two, this is One," Servius radioed, banking his *Tarpon*. "Let's get out of here before they launch some better forwards."

"Agreed One, glad to see you're still with us as well," Two replied. "Would make things a bit awkward back on deck."

Servius laughed in his mask.

Yes, yes, I suppose it would, he thought, then looked at his watch. *Not that we may have much deck left in a matter of hours.*

No. 885 Squadron Ready Room
0435 Local
H.M.C.S. Illustrious

"This plan sounds quite mad," a *Sea Hurricane* pilot muttered. "Since when can we count on the crabs for anything?"

The orphaned fighter pilots from *Eagle* and *Victorious* had taken over No. 885 Squadron's ready room by force. To be fair, the majority of the *Tarpon* drivers were getting one last meal before heading hurriedly to bed in anticipation of the Japanese Navy's counterattack. However, two of the room's actual owners sat against the aft bulkhead, glaring sullenly at the interlopers who had barged into the room.

"You know, I would take offense at that," Venkata began, "but I know *Hurricane* drivers are naturally sullen at their lot in life."

The pilot who had spoken thankfully did not take offense at Venkata's words. Instead, the man's face split into a smile.

"Was not aware we had any representatives from the junior service among us," he replied. "Much less those wearing the colors of the Royal Navy."

Venkata shrugged.

"My spares are all at the bottom of the bloody ocean," he replied. "Flight Lieutenant Venkata Singh, Rakshasa Leader."

*Not sure I'm happy to be the senior **Seafire** pilot aboard, but it was a rough day yesterday*, he thought, standing up to walk across the room. While the *Ark Royal* had survived, it appeared her casualties had been heavy. Moreover, there had not been time to transfer any of his brethren from the destroyers that had taken them off the heavily damaged vessel.

"Flight Lieutenant Gary McAdams," the man replied, also standing to shake Venkata's hand. "We haven't figured out our callsign, and they didn't assign us one."

"Iceberg," McAdams' companion, a fellow Flight Lieutenant, said. "Might as well go with something outrageous."

McAdams shook his head at the man.

"Fine then, Iceberg Flight it is, Jeremy," McAdams replied, bemused. He turned and "whispered" to Venkata, "You'll have to excuse him, he's not quite right ever since he came back from Germany."

Venkata raised an eyebrow.

"Long story," Owens replied, then looked at McAdams. "That's Germany by way of Norway, thank you very much."

I'm starting to wonder if the stress isn't starting to get to some of us, Venkata thought, well aware of the twitch he was actively suppressing. It had started as a minor tremor in his right thumb the previous evening as he'd been getting ready for bed. Before he'd fallen asleep, it had become a full-on nervous movement of his right arm.

"We've all been on long journeys to get here then," Venkata replied amicably. "As you can tell, I'm not exactly from Suffolk."

That brought a polite laugh from the four gathered *Sea Hurricane* pilots plus the other five *Seafire* pilots in the room.

"All joking aside, aren't we a bit far out of reach for your fellow *Spitfire* pilots to reach us?" McAdams asked. "I know the *Seafire* has shorter legs than that new Mark IX, but I didn't think there was *that* much of a difference."

"That's because they won't be flying *Spitfires*, gentlemen," a voice answered from the hatchway.

The pilots all turned to see an RAF Wing Commander standing in the doorway, clutching a bunch of index cards in his right hand while the other held an attache case. A tall, burly man, the officer saw that he had everyone's attention, then continued.

"I'm Wing Commander Frye, head of the fighter defenses from Gan airbase in Addu," their new visitor stated. Frye set the index cards on the table, then opened the attache case.

"According to your commanders, we haven't much time," he stated. "These cards hold the call signs and type of aircraft for the fighter support we are sending up for the navy."

Venkata shared a look with McAdams, then turned to Frye.

"Sir, what fighter support is reaching out this far?" he asked.

"I was getting to that," Frye snapped, giving Venkata a withering look. "If you will hold all questions to the end, this will go much smoother."

Well, I can see we've got a wonderful individual here, Venkata thought as he nodded. Frye studied him for an extra moment as if curious about Venkata's insignia, then set about pulling out a set of drawings.

"These are recognition drawings for the aircraft that will be supporting you," Frye continued, pointing first to a familiar outline to Venkata. "I am sure some of you are familiar with the *Beaufighter*."

"Yes, sir," Venkata stated, joined by several other pilots' affirmation. Frye once more gave him a dubious look but continued on.

"The other twin-engine aircraft is the Americans' P-38 *Lightning*," Frye stated. "The type has been quite active with our forces out of northern Australia. These are the first that have been given to the RAF."

Oh, that could be a problem, Venkata thought. *Neophyte pilots on their first combat mission with a type while over the open water....*

"You seem concerned, Mr...." Frye said, causing Venkata to jump. He realized the man was watching him intently.

I recognize that tone, Venkata thought resignedly. *Believe it or not, I really am not just some backward curry muncher.*

"Flight Lieutenant Singh," he said, drawing a look of astonishment from Frye.

"You're out of uniform, Singh," Frye stated.

"Yeah, tends to bloody happen when one's carrier gets sunk," Owens snapped, causing Frye to turn his gaze to him. The wing commander looked like he was about to say something, then thought better of it as he gazed around the room.

"Right," he said, turning back to the photos. "In any case, the intent is to rotate two flights of *Lightnings*, two of *Beaufighters*, and one of *Thunderbolts* over this force starting at dawn. Rear Admiral Vian assured my commander that the Japanese would be here no later than noon, so we should not have to worry about a second set of rotations."

Venkata looked at his watch, then the paper in his hand.

"Assuming the Japanese launch just before dawn, we'll probably have trade here in the next two hours, sir," Venkata said, resignedly.

"Trade, hmm?" Frye replied. "You sound as if you've done this before, Flight Lieutenant Singh."

The man's tone indicated he did not, in fact, believe Singh had 'done this before.'

"Every man in this compartment got in a scrap yesterday, wing commander," McAdams said. "From what the intel officers say, Flight Lieutenant Singh got three kills yesterday. Which means he's officially an ace."

Singh turned to look at McAdams in shock.

Bastard knew the whole time I was RAF, he thought, giving the other pilot a glare.

"I often play doggo, lad," McAdams said with a smile. "Makes it easier to pull people's leg."

Frye looked at Venkata with slight skepticism.

"It's a long way from Darwin, sir," Venkata said with a shrug. "Hope to bag a couple more today."

Frye's look changed from skepticism to speculation.

"How long did you say your detachment to the Fleet Air Arm was?" the man asked.

"I don't think we were given a firm end date, sir," Venkata replied. "Just that we'd see what arrangements were necessary the next time *Ark Royal* returned to port."

Or we died in the cockpit, but let's not talk about that right now, Venkata thought. Before anyone could say another word, the Tannoy interrupted them.

"Wing Commander Frye to the flag bridge," the loudspeaker crackled. "I say again, Wing Commander Frye to the flag bridge."

Frye looked upward in annoyance.

"Well, I've dallied too long here after talking to the other chaps," Frye stated. "The index cards are cheat sheets with the call signs for the respective flights. On the off chance you find yourself about to be captured, please dispose of that card in the ocean."

"In the ocean?" McAdams asked, incredulous.

"Yes, it's not waterproof ink," Frye stated. "Should come right off."

"Do you have any idea how hot a *Seafire*'s cockpit gets, sir?" Venkata asked. Frye looked at him, nonplussed.

"I would not think I'd have to tell *you* how to deal with heat," the man replied, then turned to the others. "Good luck, gentleman. God save the Queen."

"God Save the Queen," the gathered group reflexively responded. They watched as the wing commander turned and left, closing the attache case as he went.

"What an arse," McAdams said, his tone far from quiet as

Frye turned the corner out the hatch. Venkata half expected the wing commander to turn back around, but the other RAF officer didn't even break stride.

"Guess we know why he was out here in some backwater," Owens said quietly. "Man like that back in England probably would have a pilots' revolt."

"Interesting," Venkata replied, drawing a look from Owens.

"How so?" McAdams asked.

"Bloody idiots like him were the majority of the folks I had any experience with," Venkata replied simply. "If he thought about it, we don't need the pictures for twin-engine aircraft."

McAdams and Owens gave him a puzzled expression, then had near simultaneous cognition.

"Can you imagine taking kites that size off of a carrier?" Owens remarked. "You're right, it should have been abundantly obvious."

"Man's taking a twin-engine anything off a carrier, he's probably either got balls of steel or brains of mush," McAdams seconded.

Venkata shrugged.

"I submit those two conditions are not exclusive," he thought, reaching for an index card. "But, in any case, I'm heading towards my *Seafire*."

Venkata looked at the gathered group.

"Good hunting, all of you," he said. "May we all distinguish ourselves today."

"First drink is on me back in Sydney," McAdams said. "There's a lovely pub run by some Digger's widow."

"I thought Mrs. Queery's husband was missing, not dead," Owens stated, looking over at McAdams.

"He was on Malta when the Germans stormed it," McAdams replied.

"Oh," Owens said. "Well, that's unfortunate."

Venkata looked between the two men.

"Allegedly the Germans gave the island a last chance to

surrender or threatened to put every soldier to the sword," Owens explained. "Lovely blokes, those Germans."

"I imagine that violates all sorts of treaties," Venkata stated, aghast.

"Yes, well, given Her Majesty's been toying with issuing a proclamation that declares all subjects fighting for that idiot in Buckingham Palace as traitors to the realm, we're probably not going to be much better."

"Pilots, man your planes," the Tannoy crackled. "I say again, pilots, man your planes."

"They're singing our song, mates," Owens said, gesturing to the hatch. "Don't want to keep our partners waiting now, do we?"

5
...REAPING WOE

Quintili Vare, legiones redde! [Quintilius Varus, Give me back my legions!]—**Augustus Caesar**

H.M.C.S. ILLUSTRIOUS
0845 LOCAL
INDIAN OCEAN, NORTH OF ADDU
10 AUGUST

"Sir, the *Danae* reports many radar contacts, bearing oh seven oh relative her position, range seventy-five miles, heading one seven zero true."

Baines took a deep, calming breath as Rear Admiral Vian's staff sprang into action.

"Wing Commander Frye, guess you win the pool," Rear Admiral Vian said, gesturing towards a large grease board tacked to the compartment's aft bulkhead. 'ESTIMATED TIME OF STRIKES' was written across the top, with 'BUY IN £3' in slightly smaller text underneath.

Well, so much for my abilities to predict the Japanese, Baines thought, smiling as several other men cursed across the compartment. *Then again, I only missed it by a half hour.*

"I think I'd like to take my winnings and depart, Rear Admiral Vian," Frye choked out.

That man looks like he's about to be the guest of honor for a Texas hanging, Baines thought, watching the senior RAF officer swallowing. Before Vian could reply, Frye turned and vomited into a nearby trash can.

Hell of a way to make an impression, Baines thought, his own stomach doing a flip flop at the stench. *Then again, I don't blame him, as this is probably about the be the worst place to be standing for a couple hundred miles.*

"*Danae* reports that the shadowing aircraft appears to be departing the area and the strike is headed towards her," the talker near the plot reported. "She is vectoring Hammer, Mace, Arclight, and Elmo groups to attack."

Here's where we find out just how good those RAF pilots are, Baines thought, glancing at the map. *Also just how badly the Japanese want to keep chasing this task force versus settling for **Ark Royal**.*

The Japanese snoopers had arrived near the respective task forces roughly two hours before. Rear Admiral Vian had ordered the first group of float planes shot down, knowing that that act in and of itself would clue the Japanese to where the *Ark Royal* was. Unfortunately, he'd been stuck with the choice of husbanding his few remaining fighters for the main strike or launching them to chase individual reconnaissance aircraft.

*Shame that **Ark Royal** has a massive arrow pointing right at her with that oil slick*, Baines thought, fighting to keep his face calm.

"I hope Vice Admiral Fletcher appreciates the bill we are about to pay," Vian observed quietly.

Vice Admiral Fletcher had belatedly communicated his position via the U.S.S. *Curtiss* and a code relay shortly before dawn.

"Sir, if my compatriots do their job this morning, we'll bag *all* of the Japanese carriers," Baines stated, leaning on his right hand while pointing at the wooden ships that represented Fletcher with his left. "With two fast battleships, a battlecruiser, and all the other escorting ships out front, anything they damage the surface boys will catch."

"That's cold comfort for the *Victorious* and *Eagle*," someone muttered. Baines closed his eye and counted to five before responding.

"I did not say I agreed with his plan," Baines replied. "But if the Japanese launched as heavy a strike as they did yesterday, they're about to lose a whole bunch of aviators. I can assure you firsthand that cripples a fleet."

"We're not going to have a Parliamentary debate, gentlemen," Vian said firmly, looking over his staff with a cold gaze. The implied admonition not to be rude did not need to be spoken.

There's going to be a lot of bitter blood about this for decades, Baines thought. *God I hope Fletcher pulls this mousetrap off.*

"I apologize, sir," Frye said, breaking the tense silence as he drank another glass of water.

"Not a problem, wing commander," Vian replied. "It's not exactly a calm sea today."

Baines couldn't have agreed with the British admiral more. Although the sky had less cloud cover than the previous day, the *Illustrious* was definitely pitching with significant swells.

"I wish I could blame only the sea, sir," Frye replied sheepishly. "One of the reasons I joined the RAF rather than the Navy was due to being a poor swimmer."

Vian smiled at Frye's confession as the man continued.

"Thus you can understand my strong aversion to large bodies of water."

The RAF officer gestured outside the window.

"It was bad enough they sent me to a bloody island," the man said with a laugh. "But to stick me out here on a carrier in the middle of a naval battle?"

The man's expression and delivery caused a few laughs and chuckles.

"I expect to have strong words with my Member of Parliament," Frye said. "Very strong words."

Have to admire a man's cheekiness in the face of possible imminent death, Baines thought, his own face splitting into a grin.

"We will endeavour to keep you from having to use your limited skills," Vian replied, then was interrupted again by the talker.

"Enemy raid appears to be approximately one hundred aircraft. Fighters engaging now."

"Just how good of the odds do you think they'll have," Vian asked, turning to Frye.

"The only reason there are four flights out there right now is it was close to change over," Frye replied grimly, then took a breath. "The *Lightnings* will be able to stay and fight. The *Thunderbolts* are probably making one pass, then try and find the *Sunderland* to go home."

Vian turned to his chief of staff.

"Let's start reinforcing our own CAP," Vian stated. "I can only hope that's a very aggressive Japanese strike commander who will keep looking for us and not pummel poor *Ark Royal*."

Baines looked at the map.

"Sir, if it's any consolation, I'd keep heading south," the American stated, noting the range. "*Ark Royal*'s obviously a cripple and can't hurt them. But assuming the snooper saw the *Unicorn*, they'll probably want to make sure there are *no* carriers in this direction this time."

"What makes you say that?" Frye asked, genuinely curious.

"Sir, if I'd spent my entire previous night being harassed by torpedo bombers, I'd assume tonight they'd actually be carrying torpedoes," Baines said. "Our opponent turned away yesterday rather than killing this vessel. He won't make that mistake again."

Vian regarded Baines coolly.

"That is a very clinical description of what could be our imminent destruction," Vian said, then turned to his signals officer. "Turn on the homing beacon."

"Sir?" the man asked, appearing confused.

"If we are to be the stalking horse for Vice Admiral Fletcher, we might as well do our part to aid in him burning the wolves' den," Vian said simply, then turned to Frye. "It will also give any RAF chaps short of fuel a place to ditch."

Vian is as bold as his reputation, Baines thought with no small degree of terror.

The *Illustrious*' deck shifted under his feet as the carrier turned into the wind. The first of her orphan aircraft, a *Seafire*, began trundling down the deck.

"That reminds me, sir," Frye said, still looking quite green. "I met an Indian officer belowdecks who stated he was RAF despite being in an RN uniform."

"Yes, Flight Lieutenant Singh," Vian said, then raised an eyebrow. "I trust you understand why he was technically out of uniform."

"I explained it to him, sir," Commander Flint stated before Frye could answer. "Also, that you were considering mentioning him in dispatches."

It was Frye's turn to have a mildly surprised expression.

"I was wondering if you would support writing him up for a possible brevet promotion," Frye said with a nod. "One of the items we in the Commonwealth have been discussing is how to...*persuade* our Asian population to perhaps rally to Her Majesty's forces."

Vian considered what Frye had said for a few moments.

"I think that Flight Lieutenant Singh, at least according to our intelligence officers, has earned a brevet promotion," Vian said. "That it will perhaps help Her Majesty to gain us further forces will be a bonus."

Baines listened as the talker detailed a couple of RAF flights breaking off contact to head for home. Frye listened with pursed lips, checking the cheat sheet he'd brought with him to the bridge.

"Turning on the beacon might have been a good plan," he said. "There is one *Thunderbolt* flight that hasn't reported breaking off."

*Here's to hoping it's because they're overstaying their welcome and **not** because the flight leader is dead*, Baines thought grimly.

"Sir, we have two more flights approaching."

"What?" Frye and Vian asked simultaneously.

"Meteor and Comet flights, sir," the talker replied nervously.

"They're early," Frye stated, eyes narrowing. "Someone back at Gan gambled."

"How long until they are overhead?" Vian asked.

"Ten minutes, sir," the talker stated, listening to the chatter on the fighter control net.

Baines looked at the plot and did some geometry.

They'll get here just before the Japanese do, he thought, chewing his lip.

"Are *Lightnings* better at high altitude or low?" Vian asked.

"High," Frye said without hesitation. "At least, higher than you Navy types are usually fighting."

"Add them to the high cover," Vian ordered, watching as the wooden planes symbolizing the Japanese on the flag plot continued to close. "Hopefully they'll keep the dive bombers from making a mess of things."

VISHNU FLIGHT
0920 LOCAL

That's a bloody mess heading our way, Venkata thought, advancing his throttles. The sky was full of whirling aircraft, with smudges of smoke in the far distance. Closer in, two of the large *Thunderbolt* fighters went hurtling by him, one trailing smoke and clearly damaged. Roughly a half mile behind them were two *Lightnings* and a *Beaufighter*. Then beyond that…

"Tally ho, lads," Venkata said, charging his guns. "Let us get after them."

For their part, the six Japanese fighters chasing the RAF quickly broke off from their intended prey and turned towards Venkata and his four companions. Beneath the six *Seafires*, the four *Sea Hurricanes* of Iceberg flight began to head towards the staggered groups of Japanese dive bombers still pressing on towards the *Illustrious*.

Good luck, Owens, Venkata thought, starting to jink his fighter as he rushed toward the first Japanese *chutai*. Having learned from the previous day, Venkata concentrated more on trying to avoid being a steady target than scoring his own kills against the big radial engine Japanese fighter. Tracers arced all around his *Seafire*, but the reassuring lack of impacts led him to believe that he'd successfully dodged. He pulled back on his stick, glancing back towards Vishnu Two just in time to see his wingman and one of the Japanese fighters merge in a horrific spinning cloud of debris, propellers, and what looked vaguely like half a pilot.

Bloody hell, Venkata thought, glancing the other way to see the remaining two Japanese rolling their fighters back toward him. He spun his fighter and was about to bring his nose back down when suddenly there were many, many impacts aft on his fuselage.

"Wait your goddamn turn!" he shouted, seeing the offending Japanese fighter flash by. Before it could come around, a concentrated stream of tracer fire sliced off its wing. Its assailant, an RAF *Lightning*, continued underneath Venkata's *Seafire* towards the approaching bombers as well.

I owe someone a drink, he thought, then whipped his head around to try and find his original foes. He did find both of the *Shinden*, the lead aircraft having latched onto a limping *Beaufighter*. Just as Venkata started his attack run, the Japanese pilot fired a quick burst that destroyed the *Beaufighter*'s remaining engine, sending the RAF aircraft tumbling out of the sky. Like a good wingman, the second *Shinden* turned into Venkata's attack while warning his leader of the impending danger.

I hate head on runs, Venkata thought, this time bracing himself to accept whatever happened. As the *Shinden*'s wings flashed, he squeezed his own trigger. Thankfully his aim was truer, the enemy fighter staggering then starting to flip into a stall as they flashed by one another. Venkata had a momentary image of a shattered cockpit before he was kicking his rudder and looking for the original flight leader.

Oh fuck, he thought, seeing the approaching *Shinden* way too late to do anything about its attack run. The four streams of cannon shells suddenly ripped into his *Seafire*, the explosions and fragments ripping through the fighter's frame. With a dull *whoomph!*, Venkata was suddenly surrounded by an orange cocoon of flame as the fighter's fuel tanks ignited.

Get out! Gotta get out!

Despite his panicked thoughts and dire situation, Venkata moved with practiced alacrity. Much to his fellow pilot's mockery, he had practiced escaping from a *Spitfire* every evening while stationed near Darwin. Now, even as the flames licked at his protective gear and across his face, he went through the practiced movements. First, the canopy came off. Then, the seatbelts. Finally, he brought the stick over to roll the fighter onto its back. Getting no response from the descending aircraft, he stood up into the slipstream, then kicked off the side of the fuselage.

Please don't be on fire, please don't be on fire, Venkata thought, tumbling as he tried to look back at his parachute. Satisfied he wasn't going to be a flaming comet, Venkata spread his arms and legs in an attempt to stop his wild tumble. The sound of cannon fire and tracers arcing by him led to his looking up just in time to see a Japanese fighter trying to come around for him.

You asshole! Venkata thought, watching as the *Shinden* began to come around. Justice was swift, however, as a *Lightning* jumped the enemy fighter from behind. Two bursts and the *Shinden* started to follow what remained of Venkata's *Seafire* down toward the Indian Ocean below.

Oh shit, need to pull my chute, Venkata thought, then put deed to action. White hot agony seared through him as the lower straps jerked harshly into his groin.

That's why they always warned us about strap placement,

Venkata thought, struggling not to vomit while making frantic adjustments. Confident that he still had two functional testicles, he looked back towards the task force. Black puffs of fire were already appearing over the distant vessels, with matching long streaks of smoke arcing down from on high.

I hope we did enough, Venkata thought. *But I'm scared we did not.*

Venkata's fears were well founded in some ways, baseless in others. Already glancing at their fuel gauges, the Japanese strike had been about to fall upon the *Ark Royal*. In one of warfare's perverse turns, the initial RAF attack had killed the *de facto* strike commander, the commander of *Hiryu*'s dive bomber squadron. The ensuing scrap had further discombobulated the dive bombers and fighters, with several of the former breaking away from the *Ark Royal*. The latter, comprising primarily the older *Zeroes*, struggled to survive against the RAF, never mind actually protecting their charges. It was only the specter of fuel starvation and the low number of RAF fighters that had prevented the *Kido Butai*'s strike from largely coming apart over the *Ark Royal*.

In the end, it would be the *Soryu*'s new torpedo squadron commander, Lieutenant Commander Jurou Akio, who rallied what fighters he could and took the *Kido Butai*'s main strength south. With most of the CAP engaged with what few *Shinden* had accompanied the group and the reinforcing RAF fighters arriving just as the torpedo bombers reached their initial points, Akio's gamble paid off. Barely.

GALLERY DECK
H.M.C.S. ILLUSTRIOUS
0930 LOCAL

"I must say, it would appear that our opponents certainly know how to pull off a coordinated strike!" Barker shouted, the banging of *Illustrious*' anti-aircraft guns making the words barely audible.

Servius did not deign to reply as he continued to study the onrushing torpedo bombers through his binoculars. *Illustrious* shuddered from a near miss aft, the 1,000-lb bomb far wide from the rapidly maneuvering carrier.

"Stretcher parties aft! Stretcher parties aft!" the Tannoy rang out, its call indicating the two near misses preceding the wide bomb had produced splinter damage.

Servius and Barker stood in the gallery deck that lined the *Illustrious*' flight deck just forward of the island. Ostensibly part of a damage control party, both men had mutually agreed they didn't want to be inside the hull if the carrier was hit. *Victorious*' death throes had been recounted by the few of her pilots who had escaped, and Bies One's crew intended to be over the side well before that happened.

It's not cowardice if it's based on experience, Servius thought, exalting as he saw one of the distant torpedo bombers explode in a puff of smoke. He had only counted six on *Illustrious*' starboard side but was not sure how many others assailed the carrier from port.

"Bloody good formation," Barker breathed in professional admiration as the five remaining enemy aircraft wheeled as if on a string. Tracers reached out towards the quintet, and Servius was suddenly aware of the *Prince of Wales* coming up from abaft of the *Illustrious* as the carrier began turning to port. With a concussive force, the battleship's main battery sent ten shells arcing toward the charging Japanese.

That never bloody works, you idiots, Servius thought angrily... then ate his words as the line of waterspouts smashed one of the approaching bombers over onto its back. The Japanese pilot had no time to correct his aircraft's path before it smashed into the ocean in another waterspout.

"Bloody good shot!" Barker shouted, whooping like a fan at a soccer pitch. Servius was about to join him when there was the roar of a propeller approaching fast from astern. Without looking, Servius grabbed Barker and crouched for the deck. His instincts were rewarded a moment later as a dark green shape flashed overhead, the torpedo bomber's rear gunner firing wildly back toward *Illustrious* as the plane continued away. Bullets ricocheting off the carrier's side were followed by at least two screams, one rising horribly in intensity.

That's not good, Servius had time to think just before his ears were assaulted by the sound of the collision alarm. assaulted his ears. Once again, instincts saved him as he threw himself flat to the deck shortly before it whipped upward and to the side. The sound of several ankles breaking around him was audible, followed shortly by exclamations of pain and anger.

That's even worse, Servius thought, bracing himself as *Illustrious* continued into her turn. Looking out from the vessel's side, he saw the *Unicorn* heeled over hard to port in the distance, dark shapes flying through the skies around her. A few seconds passed, then there was one torpedo to starboard...and another trio in quick succession to port.

She's done for, Servius thought, feeling sick to his stomach as the other vessel began to slow, already listing towards the more grievous wounds to port.

"I think that's the end of her," Barker breathed beside him. Servius unconsciously nodded in agreement at the Canadian's assessment. As if to further accentuate Barker's point, there was a brilliant gout of flame from the *Unicorn*'s aft end as her petrol storage ignited. Before their horrified eyes, the entire stern of the carrier rapidly turned into a cauldron of hell on earth, bright orange jets visible even from their perch. Briefly, Servius considered raising the glasses around his neck...then thought better of it.

"You lot, are you fit?" someone shouted. "If so, stop gawking and come lend a hand!"

Servius turned to see the speaker was a young Chief Petty Officer. The NCO's eyes widened as he realized just who he'd been addressing. Servius gave him a disarming smile as he headed in the direction the man was pointing.

"Sorry my good man, was just regarding some unfathomable horrors," Barker said from behind him, his voice sounding strained as they passed into the *Illustrious'* hangar deck. Servius caught himself as he started to trip.

She's down by the head and listing to starboard slightly, he thought, assessing the area in front of him. *Nothing like poor* **Unicorn**, *so we might make it out of this yet.*

As if on cue, the carrier's heavy anti-aircraft guns gave a final ragged salvo, the sound of roaring engines fading into the distance.

"Grab some of the shoring material as you go past!" another petty officer shouted ahead of them. "Follow Chief Petty Officer Sims in the red vest!"

Not sure that's the best use of flight deck crew outfits, Servius thought, then had a chilling thought. *That is unless that's someone up from a magazine and that's where we're headed.*

Roughly five minutes later, Servius was pleased to note that it was not, in fact, a magazine bulkhead that needed shoring. *Illustrious* had taken the fish barely five feet back from the bow. After another twenty soaking wet, hot minutes working under the haphazard lighting of battle lanterns, Servius and Barker's damage control party had managed to stuff enough wooden blocks and other material into the myriad holes before them to largely stop any further spread of water.

"Yes sir, we can resume speed," Servius heard Chief Petty Officer Sims speaking into a sound-powered telephone. There was a long pause filled with the heavy, labored breathing of about twenty men undercut by the sloshing of a large quantity of water up to their knees.

It is downright eerie hearing this sound, knowing there are many more tons of water on the other side of that bulkhead, Servius thought, glancing nervously forward where the watertight hatches gave the occasional groan of straining metal. *Good thing she's a newer vessel. Can't imagine what it'd be like aboard* **Warspite** *or some other decrepit old wench trying to stop damage like this.*

"The pumps seem to be getting ahead of it, sir," Sims continued, turning the battle lantern around the dim compartment. "I'll get a sounding and let you know."

There was a long pause, then Sims nodded at something said on the other end.

"Aye-aye, sir, I'll ask," Sims said. The petty officer then held the phone down to his chest before calling out into the compartment, "Are there any air group folks about?"

Servius looked at Barker, then back at Sims.

"Yes," they both answered, followed a moment later by another voice Servius didn't recognize in a different corner.

"Captain has instructed all of you to return to your respective ready rooms, sir," Sims said, looking at Servius. "Unless you happen to be Commander Ellis."

Oh this is just lovely, Servius thought. *I wonder what the hell is going on now? Did Fletcher's task force get eaten alive by a sea monster?*

"Why, it just happens that I am," Servius said, sloshing towards Sims.

"You're wanted in the flag plot, sir," Sims replied lowly once Servius was within close earshot. "Rear Admiral Vian's orders."

Servius nodded, then turned to Barker.

"Looks like our work is never done, doesn't it?" he asked grimly. "Well, let's be about it."

With that, the two men began the long trek from the depths of *Illustrious*' bow to the lofty heights of the flag bridge. Roughly halfway there, Servius realized the carrier was vibrating slightly, clearly at speed.

"Hope the repairs hold," Barker observed from behind him, indicating the junior officer had also realized the vessel was pushing herself. Before Servius could reply, there was the *thud* and tremor of an aircraft landing.

"Guess that explains why we're risking it," Servius noted,

once again resuming their journey. "Be a horrible way to lose all our airborne fighters."

Barker glanced at his watch, then made a disgusted face.

"Well, I would love to do a comparison of how long we were down there compared to the fighters' endurance," the junior officer said, holding up his wrist. "But it would appear that a certain watchmaker on Savile Row lied to me about the 'absolute watertight integrity' of this watch."

Servius winced.

"I hope it wasn't too costly for you," he replied, then smiled. "Of course, perhaps now that bloke is giving German pilots substandard timepieces at a discount."

Barker gave his superior a grim smile as they resumed their journey.

"One could only hope," the man replied as they reached *Illustrious'* Gallery Deck once more.

"Sir, please don't let them talk us into any more insane long searches in the dark," Barker pleaded. "I'm starting to see that radar scope in my waking hours, and it is not a pleasant view."

"I make no promises, Barker," Servius replied. Once more, he was interrupted by the noise of a landing aircraft, this one's engine sounding like a poorly maintained washing machine.

"What the hell is wrong with that plane?" Barker asked, concerned.

"I imagine he's taken a bit of damage," Servius observed. "Has to have been a hell of a scrap up there. But given we avoided a massacre like yesterday, it would appear the fighters got the upper hand."

Barker reached up towards his pocket, then stopped.

"Goddammit," he said, dropping his hand to his side. "They're likely soaked."

"Reasonably certain the smoking lamp is most definitely *out* as well," Servius replied from the base of the ladder. He looked up again as another damaged aircraft came in from astern. This one landed with a much harder impact, and both men crouched as they listened to the aircraft scrape down the *Illustrious'* armored deck.

"Medical team to the flight deck! Medical team to the flight deck!" the Tannoy sounded. The rush of feet a few paces away spurred Servius to continue on his task. With a final wave, he left Barker and finished his climb up to the island.

"Here's the man we've all been waiting for," Rear Admiral Vian said by way of greeting as Servius walked through the door.

I guess that did take a bit longer than it should have, Servius thought, nodding toward the superior officer. There were several odd looks, and Servius belatedly realized he was the only one still wearing his steel helmet.

"Guess I don't need this anymore," he said hopefully, looking around the compartment. The gathered group seemed particularly in a good mood, with smiles on most of their faces.

"No, no, you shouldn't," Vian replied, gesturing towards the map. "It would appear that the Americans paid a visit to our assailants whilst the strike group was attacking us."

Servius moved eagerly to look at the map. He noted that there were two wooden markers with a black "X" on them, with another two having hash marks.

"Unless Fletcher is particularly slow, he'll bag the whole lot of them," Vian said, gesturing to where an Allied surface group appeared to be a little over a hundred miles away from the Japanese carriers.

Almost worth it if Rear Admiral Vian is right, he thought. *If Fletcher gets all six of their big carriers, surely they'll call off the invasion.*

"In any case, that's not why I called you up here," Vian said, breaking Servius' gaze at the table. "I need you to get with the staff and devise a plan for keeping ASW aircraft over the *Ark Royal* tonight."

Servius nodded.

"I can make that happen, sir," he replied. "Don't want to

give the Japanese a chance to snatch some solace from the beating they're apparently receiving."

Vian gave him a wry smile.

"Well, we'll see if American aviators can count any better than you lot," Vian replied. "I remember many times we thought we'd hit an Italian vessel with several torpedoes only to find out we missed completely."

Servius shrugged.

"When do you want the patrols to start, sir?" he asked.

"We should be able to keep *Sunderlands* around her for the rest of the day," the RAF wing commander standing to Vian's rear stated. Servius noted the man looked positively stricken with some sort of malady, holding onto the back of a chair like it was a cane.

Hope whatever he has isn't catching, Servius thought, turning back to the map.

"If you give me an hour, sir, I can work something up," Servius replied.

There was another crash from the flight deck, followed by the alarm for a fire.

"That is if the fighter boys don't break the carrier."

6

REPAIRS AND RECONSTITUTION

Ships...must have secure ports to which to return, and must be followed by the protection of their country through the voyage—
Alfred Thayer Mahan

GAN AIRBASE
ADDU ATOLL
0845 LOCAL
13 AUGUST

"I never thought I'd be so happy to see a carrier getting towed into a harbor," Wing Commander Frye observed wearily. The RAF officer stood along Addu's shore in his tropical white uniform, his pale legs almost a visibility hazard.

Venkata looked over at the superior officer with a wry smile. The two men were standing on the opposite side of the atoll from the throng of humanity that was currently cheering the *Ark Royal*'s entrance into safe harbor.

I misjudged him based on our single meeting, Venkata thought, turning back toward the carrier. His bandaged hands were throbbing, a sure indicator that he should have taken pain pills long before now, but he had not wanted to miss the carrier's arrival.

We all managed to keep you alive, Shilling Base, Venkata

thought, a wave of melancholy sweeping over him. *Even if that butcher's bill was quite steep.*

Ark Royal had been hit by another two bombs during the IJN's final strike. Physically neither weapon had done any real further damage to the crippled carrier. Their effect on the crew, however, was far more devastating. Over one hundred men had been killed by the two hits, with most of the casualties occurring among the aircrew trapped onboard by the carrier's inability to steam. Among the dead were Squadron Leader Marshall and almost every other *Seafire* pilot who hadn't been in the air.

"The doctors tell me it's going to be another three weeks before you'll be fit to fly," Frye stated conversationally. "I'll give you some time to think on it, but I'd like to rotate you back to Sydney to fall in on some of the new aircraft."

"Sir, I'd prefer to stay out here if you don't mind," Venkata replied earnestly.

"With those burns?" Frye asked, nodding towards Venkata's arms and hands. "There's a decent chance you'll end up infected."

Venkata's response was interrupted by the roar of four P-47s flying just over their heads. The massive American-built fighters waggled their wings as they passed over the atoll, drawing ever louder cheers from the men gathered across it.

"Sir, I checked with the doctors," Venkata replied. "They say as long as I change the dressings regularly and don't do anything stupid like try to swim in the ocean, I should be fine."

"I assure you, we won't be seeing any *Spitfires* or *Seafires* out this way for a while," Frye pointed out. "Especially with the *Unicorn* gone."

"I cannot believe the Americans aren't even offering to shuttle fighters from Australia after Fletcher's cock up," Venkata spat bitterly.

Frye shook his head.

"From the Americans' perspective, it was a great victory," the wing commander replied, holding up one hand. He then raised his other. "Of course, from Her Majesty's and the Navy's perspective, this was a horrible defeat. The Japanese not only sank almost all of our modern carriers, they also took Ceylon to boot."

After a spirited defense, Ceylon's garrison had yielded to the inevitable once it was clear the United States Navy wasn't interested in fighting the invasion fleet. The island garrison had surrendered the day before, and Venkata could not help but think of Owens' discussion about how the Axis had treated prisoners at Malta.

"It's a bloody disgrace, and Her Majesty's Empire shrinks by the day," Frye said, voice thick with emotion as he turned north.

Oh yes, there's that galling pill to swallow, Venkata thought, lips pressed together so he didn't say something untoward. *Leave it to an imperialist to be more upset about the loss of some "empire" than the thousands of dead sailors.*

"At least the Japanese losses mean Australia is safe," Venkata noted, reaching towards his itchy arms before stopping. "Between their losses in aircraft and ships, I doubt they have the wherewithal to even think about coming south."

Frye harumphed at that.

"I suppose it's easier for you to look at the bright side," the wing commander said. "You have far more faith in the Americans seeing this through than I do."

Venkata couldn't stop himself from letting out a short laugh.

"Something amusing?" Frye asked, his tone dangerous.

"Sir, the Americans *loathe* the Japanese," Venkata said, ignoring the man's imminent anger. "You would think the Japanese sucker punched them on holiday or something with how relentlessly angry some of their lot are."

Frye regarded him with disbelief.

"Perhaps at your level it seems that way," he said. "But you don't see the reports that we are provided weekly. Many

Americans are having trouble seeing why this war concerns them."

"That may be the opinion of the folks who have the luxury of an ocean around them," Venkata replied with a shrug. "But at the sharp end, they want to see this thing through."

Frye did not reply, simply turning and looking out to where a tugboat was moving the *Ark Royal* toward where a floating crane was moored.

I do hope we don't have a typhoon hit while that thing is anywhere near inhabited buildings, Venkata thought, a slight shudder going through his frame. *Besides attracting lighting, it looks horrifically unstable.*

"If you stay, you'll have to qualify on one of the new American aircraft," Frye said, turning to face Venkata.

"Sir?" Venkata asked, cursing at the slight tremble in his voice.

"I do not think burns make you hard of hearing, Singh," Frye replied. Venkata fought to keep his face passive but obviously failed.

"Yes, I know, the *Thunderbolt* is a flying abomination passing as a juggernaut, and the *Lightning* is what happens when you let engineers run amok," Frye continued, quoting some of the more derisive comments *Spitfire* and *Hurricane* pilots had made about their American-built counterparts. "But again, there are no more of our fighters coming this way for weeks, if not months."

Venkata started to clasp his hands together in front of him, then stopped.

Well, at least that nervous tic will get broken by the time these bandages come off, he thought grimly.

"Sir, then I guess I'll have to take my leave of his place," Venkata said, shoulders slumping. "I just feel that this is going to become a hotbed as we move more forces in here."

Frye smiled, gesturing towards where American Seabees were busy expanding Gan base.

"While I do not think you are wrong," Frye replied with a

smile, "that's just one more reason we're not bringing any *Spitfires* here. This is about to become a battle of long-range attrition with Ceylon."

That's a lot of water to fly over, Venkata thought, thinking back to his time in a dinghy after bailing out.

The *Illustrious'* screen and the *Sunderlands* had rescued many of the friendly fighter pilots who'd been shot down. However, after a couple of incidents, they'd left at least two dozen Japanese pilots to their fate. Four of *those* men had "reconsidered their views on being captured," in the dry words of one *Sunderland* pilot. It was the handful of bodies that the *Sunderland* and *Catalina* crews had hauled out of the water that reinforced Venkata's decision to go back to Australia.

Don't blame the one chap they found with a Nambu in his mouth and his brains all over the back of his raft, Venkata mused.

"Surely there will need to be some sort of defensive effort, sir," Venkata replied incredulously. "There's not a better interceptor than the *Spitfire*."

"The *Lightning* pilots would beg to differ," Frye replied. "In any case, it's close enough that I can't hold a dozen *Spitfires* here when I could have a dozen *Lightnings* in their place. It's a matter of provisions more than anything else."

Frye reached into his pocket.

"But since you've more or less decided that you'll head back to Australia," the wing commander said with a smile, "there's something else that seems appropriate to tell you."

Venkata took an unconscious step backward, causing Frye's smile to broaden.

"Oh, this is good news, *Squadron Leader* Singh," Frye replied, extending his hand and opening it to reveal new rank insignia.

Venkata felt his heart starting to race.

"Sir, I..." he began, taking another step back.

"You've earned it, Singh," Frye said, his face set. "Not only did you volunteer to fly out and help the Navy, but you also conducted yourself above and beyond almost every pilot out there."

"T-t-thank you, sir," Venkata stuttered, reaching out to take the rank.

"It's not effective until the 15th," Frye stated, putting the insignia in his hand. "There's a destroyer departing for Australia tomorrow morning. My adjutant will provide you with details as well as message traffic. Say any goodbyes you have to and make sure you're on it."

"Yes, sir," Venkata choked out. He fought to keep tears of happiness from welling up as he saluted Frye. The Wing Commander returned the gesture, and Venkata immediately began heading towards his hut to prepare.

Father, mother, I have done you proud, he thought, finally letting his emotions overwhelm him. *I will continue to serve Her Majesty in the way you taught me.*

COMMAND POST WHITBY
0220 LOCAL
15 SEPTEMBER

"I will say this for our opponents," Barker observed from the other side of the map, "they are bloody persistent."

It was oppressively hot inside the darkened, blacked out hut. Located on a small outcropping just off the north end of Gan's runway, the facility had been thrown up with its primary focus being on function rather than form. As a command post, that meant it was wonderfully equipped with radar relays, tactical boards, and radios. On the other hand, its habitability was questionable at best, with the only saving grace being that the light not getting out made it extremely hard for any unwanted insects to get in.

Hard but not impossible, Servius thought, smashing a mosquito that had alighted on his arm. Making sure the insect was well and truly dead, he wiped his brow and considered the contact that had elicited Barker's comment.

I don't think I will know what Barker looks like in normal light soon, Servius thought, glancing at his watch. *While I agree these red bulbs are great for night vision, it just seems so bloody surreal to come here in darkness, spend all night in red, then head to the shacks in the gloom.*

"You would think that they'd eventually realize surfacing at night seems to be lethal," the commander stated. According to the American *Catalina* that had spotted the submarine, it had been cruising roughly seventy miles northwest of Addu Atoll. The *Catalina*, Tucson 44, was reasonably sure it was a Japanese I-boat, but the outline had seemed strange in the flares' light. Unlike most pilots, the American was also almost certain he'd missed despite catching the submarine by surprise.

From the description, seems like it might be one of those mother ships, Servius thought, taking a sip of a canteen. *Which means we **definitely** need to kill it.* Apparently the Japanese had quite the fleet of midget submarines, as evidenced by the insanity that had taken place in both Sydney and Darwin.

In the month since the Battle of Ceylon's conclusion, Task Force Orca (as the group of submarine hunters had taken to calling themselves) had bagged sixteen Japanese submarines. The first four had been I-boats milling about near the graves of the *Eagle* and *Victorious*, all sailing disparate courses with seemingly no rhyme or reason. Thankfully, one of them had managed to leave two survivors, one of whom had been a Korean mess servant apparently coerced into serving on his late vessel.

Thank God we had someone who actually spoke Korean, Servius thought, chewing his lip as he listened to the chatter on the radio.

"Damn Yank is a chatty Cathy," Barker stated, obviously perturbed as he also took a drink of water.

"Lad's just excited they might have something pinned down," Servius chided his companion, glancing around the hut. "Has plenty of fuel, wants to make sure they put paid to the bastard."

"Right, but he's probably warning everyone else within fifty miles that mayhem is ensuing," Barker retorted. "It's not just the Japanese I'm worried about, and we *know* the Germans can pick up radio signals for dozens of miles on their boats."

Servius wanted to say that his backseater was being paranoid. Unfortunately, with it having been almost a month, there was more than enough time for the Italians or Germans to redirect any of their submarines that had been in the Indian Ocean towards the Maldives. In reality, submarines sitting at the pier in Taranto when the *Ark Royal* was hit would have had plenty of time to make the journey.

They need to hurry up and get that advanced torpedo boom finished, Servius thought. *Otherwise, some bastard will set their torpedoes for slow and fire a spread into the harbor.*

The Royal Navy had never intended to be a dedicated, long-term fleet anchorage. Indeed, it was only due to the Churchill government's paranoia during the Lull that Gan airbase had ever been expanded to take heavy aircraft. Now with the *Ark Royal* and *Warspite* both awaiting a repair ship, a couple of tankers and depot vessels waiting to support future offensive operations, and a handful of destroyers, destroyer escorts, and sloops passing through, the place could almost be described as "fish in a barrel."

*I didn't even realize **Warspite** had been hit during that last raid*, Servius thought, shaking his head. *She's definitely had a war...or two*. The older vessel's damage was apparently not actually crippling, but the powers that be had decided she would remain in Attu until the U.S.S. *Vulcan* arrived.

*If the rumors are true that the **Anson**, **Howe**, and **Implacable** have passed through the Suez*, Servius thought, *it might be good to have ol' "Breezy Corner" around anyway. Maybe teach those two young ladies a thing or two about respecting their elders.*

"All right, Shropshire 21 should be almost there," Barker said, looking at the time and then the ready sheet. "God bless those *Liberator* pilots, they sure do respond quickly."

"I don't know who lit a fire under the RAAF Coastal Command," Servius muttered, "but they are definitely serious about protecting the *Ark Royal*."

Barker snorted.

"With all due respect, sir, she's one of only two carriers they're likely to see for the rest of this war at the rate we're going," Barker replied. "Unless the Americans decide to send something to join *Yorktown*."

Servius started to admonish Barker for talking about ship movements, then stopped.

If there's a traitor among these ratings, they sure are a walking misuse of resources, Servius thought. *Indeed, I don't even know how they'd get their messages away. Throw them in a bottle?*

"I don't think they're calling *Yorktown* back to Pearl Harbor permanently," Servius noted. "Just with Cockatoo Island pretty packed and her apparently in dire need of a refit, it was probably time."

"It seems everyone is running out of carriers," Barker replied. "Well except those bellends in England."

Servius laughed bitterly.

"Yes, well, maybe our American friends can do something about that in the Atlantic sometime soon."

"Don't know, every time they've tried, it's gone poorly for them," Barker said, his tone forlornly. "At least we don't have to deal with glide bombs."

The radio interrupted their conversation. Servius listened to the brief exchange.

"Well, let's see how long that I-boat stays under now," Barker replied.

"If he was surfacing in the first place, I imagine he's been down most of the day," Servius replied. "Probably a bit stifling inside that boat, and his batteries are likely almost depleted."

The next hour was spent in relative silence, as everyone inside the hut listened to the other aircraft arrayed in a fan expanding from Gan airbase. There was another possible contact far to the southwest, but it had faded before the *Sunderland* had turned around.

That one concerns me, to be honest, Servius thought. Just as he was about to inquire as to how long until another aircraft could be dispatched, both Tucson 44 and Shropshire 21 reported their contact returning.

We'll have to worry about that one later, Servius said, gesturing for the duty officer logbook. He wrote a note for his successor regarding the suspicious contact to the west, then turned back to where the *Catalina* and *Liberator* were prosecuting their contact.

"Good thing it's partly cloudy out there," Barker remarked. "They'll probably be able to stalk it a little bit better since there are two of them."

"Just as long as they don't bloody collide," Servius muttered, drumming his fingers on the map.

Couldn't be me out there with a pair of big aircraft in that small of space in the dark, he thought.

Shropshire 21 announced visual contact with the submarine. A few moments later, it confirmed that the craft was indeed an I-boat. Tucson 44 offered to illuminate the I-boat, but Shropshire 21 politely declined.

"Someone's about to learn about a Leigh Light," Barker observed with a smile.

"A few dozen people," Servius replied, his own face split in an evil grin. Leigh Lights, quite common with the Commonwealth's Atlantic forces, were a relatively new systems to the Pacific. A forward facing 24-inch searchlight mounted on an aircraft's wing or nose, the Leigh performed the dual function of illuminating a surfaced submarine and blinding its bridge with its brilliance. Servius leaned forward with anticipation as the Australian *Liberator* began its run.

"Goddamn Shropshire 21, you need to warn someone you brought the sun with you!" Tucson 44's startled commander stated over the radio. There was laughter around the hut as Shropshire 21 reported weapons release.

It's the waiting that's the hardest part, Servius thought as the radios briefly fell silent.

"Tucson 44, going around for another run," Shropshire 21 reported. "Counterclockwise."

"Uh, Shropshire, I think you got him," Tucson replied. There was a pause, then the American continued. "Yeah, you definitely got him, he's on fire."

Oh that's gotta be hell on earth, Servius thought grimly. *Bad enough to be in a sinking submarine. But one whose bunkerage goes up?*

"Roger Tucson 44, we can see that now," Shropshire replied. "Whitby base, do you have any more trade?"

Servius was about to answer when the door to the hut swung open.

"Group, *attention!*" he barked, recognizing Rear...no, now *Vice* Admiral Vian.

"Sir," he said, saluting.

"My God, this place gets hotter and hotter every time I visit it," Vian remarked, stepping aside so his aide could shut the door. Servius thought he saw another officer standing outside but couldn't tell before the entryway closed.

"Last thing we need is more bodies in here," Vian noted, nodding at his aide. "How goes your plan, Commander Ellis? Are you wanted by the Japanese Navy yet?"

"Ironic you should ask, sir," Barker interjected before Servius could reply. "Commander Ellis' plan just netted us another submarine."

Vian looked at Servius in happy surprise.

"Well, I certainly chose a great night to go for a walk then," he replied. "Especially since I come bearing news."

"Sir?" Servius said.

"Your presence is requested in Sydney," Vian stated. "The Yanks are holding a Board of Inquiry over the most recent troubles, and they wanted to speak with the squadron commander who harassed our Japanese friends all night a month ago."

Vian gave Servius a mischievous grin.

"There's mutterings that they also might want to give you an award, but that's probably just a rumor," Vian replied, gesturing towards his aide. The lieutenant commander, a man Servius had never seen before, reached into his attaché bag and produced a smallish box. Vian took it as the aide finished fishing into the bag for a slip of paper.

Hope your eyes are good, mate, Servius thought. The lieutenant commander squinted as Vian continued.

"Can't have the Yanks gonging you before we do," the vice admiral stated. "Lieutenant Commander Farnsworth, publish the orders."

"Aye, aye, sir," Farnsworth said. "For conspicuous gallantry, while serving as commander of No. 819 Squadron aboard Her Majesty's Ship *Illustrious*, Commander Servius Ellis is entered into the Companions of the Distinguished Service Order...."

The remainder of the citation was lost in a rush of blood to Servius' ears. He was still in a daze as Vian attached the DSO, followed by the gathered men congratulating him. Servius could barely speak for a good five minutes, so great was his astonishment.

"Well, now that I've completely disrupted your work," Vian finished, "I'll let you get back to your predatory ways."

"T-t-thank you, sir," Servius replied, leaning on the table for support.

"As for you, Barker, we'll probably be getting you some new uniform accessories soon as well," Vian stated with a sly smile. "It would appear that your service is a bit slower in getting some paperwork done."

"Always the case, sir," Barker said with mock exasperation.

"In any case, you'll need to be at the quay for a *Sunderland* in about five hours," Vian said. "Sorry, you're going to miss the Queen's speech."

I'd forgotten all about that, Servius thought, glancing at the clock.

"Yes sir, I'll turn over things to Barker and start getting ready," Servius replied.

"The staff has already sent ahead a note on the uniform of the day," Vian said. "Hopefully, we won't have another cock up in a few months after this work is done."

I don't think our fleet can afford another incident like the last few weeks, Servius thought. *We simply don't have any more ships.*

U.S.S. ENTERPRISE
SYDNEY HARBOR
1430 LOCAL
20 SEPTEMBER

"Excuse me, Lieutenant Commander, but may I help you?"

Baines felt the color rush to his face as he regarded the Commonwealth officer in front of him. The two men had met in the small compartment outside the admiral's day cabin aboard the American carrier *Enterprise*. Baines had been unable to keep his eyes off the man after he had entered the compartment, feeling as if he'd just seen a ghost.

"My apologies, I did not mean to stare," Baines said in a rush, feeling somewhat faint. "It's just you reminded me of someone I used to know."

The British officer gave him a smile that could have flash-froze a summer lake.

"Ah, I was wondering if you were Lieutenant Commander Baines from the description I was given," the man replied, his tone icy. "I assure you, you're not seeing a specter, sir. My brother and I always bore a strong resemblance to one another."

Oh shit, Baines thought, sudden realization hitting him like a ton of bricks. *The other Commander Farmer, liaison on the* **Houston**.

"Alas, I guess we won't be playing a lark on our relatives or beguiling any young ladies while pub crawling anytime soon," the man continued. "Tell me, how well do you sleep knowing that you're directly responsible for the death of several hundred of your allies? Does the fact you were 'just following orders' keep you warm at night?"

Baines clenched his fist.

"I must say, your brother was less of a whiny bastard," he

spat, standing up from his chair. Farmer's face drained of color, and the coffee mug he'd been filling dropped from his hand to hit the deck. The man started to step towards him when the hatch opened to reveal the *Enterprise*'s executive officer, Commander John Crommelin.

"The board will..." Crommelin started, then stopped as he saw Farmer's posture. "Is there a problem, gentlemen?"

The drawled question hung in the air as Farmer and Baines stared at one another.

"No, sir, there is not on my end," Baines said slowly. Farmer continued to glare at him, nostrils flaring.

"Commander Farmer?" Crommelin asked, looking at the British officer. "Do you need another mug?"

One thing about being from the South is I recognize that thickening drawl as a very bad sign, Baines thought. *Someone here will be leaving in irons if he's not careful.*

"No, Commander Crommelin," Farmer said, his tone clipped. "I think I'll go out on deck and get some fresh air until it's time to catch that *Catalina*."

"I understand," Crommelin said, looking back and forth between Baines and Farmer. "I'll get a steward to clean up the spilled coffee."

"Thank you," Farmer said, nodding. "My apologies for the mess. It was a *pleasure* to meet you, Lieutenant Commander Baines."

*Why do I get the sensation it was anything **but** a pleasure?* Baines thought. *Unless it's a pleasure to actually lay eyes on me so he is certain who he'll be stabbing if we ever meet again.*

"Let's not keep the board waiting, Lieutenant Commander Baines," Crommelin stated. Baines nodded, watching as Farmer exited the compartment towards the flight deck in a rush. He turned back to Crommelin.

"You know, the *Houston*'s captain swears by the man," Crommelin observed. "But he's had nothing but anger and attitude since he's been aboard."

"Admiral King basically murdered his brother and a few hundred other British sailors," Baines stated, drawing a surprised look from Crommelin. "But I guess he won't be answering any questions about that, will he?"

Crommelin shared a grim smile at that one.

"No, not unless Old Scratch gives him shore leave," Crommelin stated. "But, let's get you in to Rear Admiral Spruance."

The next two hours were not exactly grueling but far from pleasant. To Baines' surprise, the Board of Inquiry seemed to be an open-minded attempt to determine what had gone wrong between Vice Admiral Fletcher and Cunningham. Rear Admiral Spruance's questions were nuanced and showed a surprising amount of understanding about carrier operations. Recognizing Captain Mitscher, the former commander of the sunk *Hornet*, as one of the board members, Baines could only assume that most of the aviation questions came from that quarter.

"Well, Lieutenant Commander Baines, we don't want to make you late for evening meal," Rear Admiral Spruance observed, glancing up at the clock on the bulkhead behind him. "We'll wrap this up by asking you for your final thoughts. The floor is yours, and what you say will have no consequences outside of this room."

Right, like I'm dumb enough to fall for that, Baines thought, keeping his face impassive. *Then again, I'm an aviation officer who has only one eye and will undoubtedly never be allowed onto one of Her Majesty's vessels again.*

"Sir, the best thing we can do for the Brits is get them another carrier," Baines said simply, drawing several glances among the board. "I know that we don't exactly have them growing like trees at Mare Island. However, I think we can all agree at this point that our CVs are as important, if not more important, than the battlewagons."

He could tell that statement didn't sit well with some of the surface officers on the board. Spruance, however, nodded and took a note.

"With the carriers we have, I think it's well past time to put more fighters onboard," Baines continued. "I've gotten a free swim twice now, and both times it was simply a case of not enough defenders when the Japanese came calling."

Baines swept his one remaining eye over the board.

"While I will, for obvious reasons, be unavailable to personally return the favor to my counterparts in the Japanese fleet," he stated angrily, "I think that with about twenty more fighters per flight deck, we're not talking about the *Victorious* and the *Eagle* in the past tense."

"You don't think the element of surprise had something to do with the two vessels' loss?" Rear Admiral Buckmaster, seated at the far end of the table, asked. The *Yorktown*'s former master, Buckmaster had been Baines' executive officer when he first reported aboard the *Lexington*. He had personally selected Baines for promotion and his transfer to the *Saratoga*.

He'd been so quiet throughout this whole thing, I wondered if I'd somehow upset him, Baines thought, mulling his answer.

"Sir, I think the storm messing with the radar didn't help," Baines replied. "But another couple of dozen fighters launched, even if they stayed at low level and had to fight the torpedo bombers, would have made a difference."

Buckmaster scribbled a note then looked back up.

"I will say that the Royal Navy is hesitant to add more aircraft to their carriers," Buckmaster observed. "This has been resisted in both the Atlantic and Pacific in the last few weeks."

"It's a matter of different deck rules, sir," Baines said. "You can tell their doctrine got formed when they had to worry about land-based bombers showing up with little warning. Which, I might add, will be advantageous if we have to fight the carrier they've allegedly moved into the Indian Ocean."

Spruance smiled at that comment.

"Well, it certainly worked with the two escort carriers Vice Admiral Fletcher caught off Africa," the flag officer replied. "But that's noted, and I'm sure Admiral Richardson will have a discussion with Vice Admiral Vian once the *Illustrious* is out of dry dock."

"Sir, if I might ask, how long do they think she'll take to repair?" Baines inquired.

"Probably another two weeks," Rear Admiral Spruance replied, then glanced at Baines speculatively. "Why do you ask?"

"Sir, as far as I know, I am still the liaison to the Far Eastern Fleet," Baines said. "While I enjoyed the two weeks survivor's leave in Canberra, I'd like to have an idea how long it will be before I go back to sea."

Spruance looked at the other officers, particularly Buckmaster.

"Actually, you're being reassigned," Buckmaster said finally. "You'll be part of my staff going forward."

Baines felt relief wash over him. Despite his best efforts, it must have shown.

"Don't be too happy," Buckmaster said. "I've been tasked by BuAir to head to Kansas and take over the Naval Air Primary Training Center at Fairfax Airport, Kansas City, Kansas."

Baines gestured at his ruined face.

"Sir, I was pretty sure I was never going to get another sea command," he said resignedly. "If I can't be the fist punching the Japanese in the face, I'm okay with helping form the fingers."

Buckmaster nodded at that.

"Then I'm glad to have you, Lieutenant Commander Baines," the rear admiral said.

Spruance once again looked at the clock.

"With that, these proceedings are closed," Spruance said. Baines and the rest of the men in the room stood, followed shortly by Spruance doing so as well. Baines heard the hatch open behind him and turned to see Commander Crommelin reentering the compartment.

"I don't know about you gentlemen, but it is my intent to

splice the mainbrace in two hours at The Fortune. Lieutenant Commander Baines, you are welcome to join us."

"Thank you, sir," Baines replied, surprised. "I will join you henceforth."

Spruance continued to lead the board out of the compartment.

"Looking forward to it," Spruance said, then nodded at Crommelin as he and the board filed out. Crommelin waited for them to leave, then sidled over to Baines.

"It's fried chicken and green beans in the wardroom tonight," Crommelin stated. "Figured you wouldn't mind getting some decent food after all those weeks with the Limeys."

Baines chuckled.

"Yes, yes, I think that would be wonderful, sir," Baines said. "It's been a trying time, to say the least."

ABOUT THE AUTHOR

James Young is an American author of science fiction, alternative history, and post-apocalyptic fiction. His primary series is the *Usurper's War*, which is set in an alternate history where Adolf Hitler is killed by an RAF bomb in November 1940.

He is also the author of *The Vergassy Chronicles*, a military sci-fi universe set in the 3050s.

In addition to his own work, James has edited anthologies including bestselling authors Sarah Hoyt, S.M. Stirling, and David Weber.

His non-fiction writing credits include *Eagles, Ravens, and Other Birds of Prey*, winning the United States Naval Institute's (USNI's) 2016 Cyberwarfare Essay Contest, and various articles in *Armor*, *The Journal of Military History*, and *Proceedings*.

There's more on the next page...

LinkTree
(i.e., one stop for everything)

https://linktr.ee/jamesyoungauthor

Blog
(i.e., the thing I wish I updated more often)

Jamesyoungauthor.com

OTHER BOOKS BY JAMES

(First In Series or Standalones)

Usurper's War Series | Has Audiobook

The Spartan Trilogy (Vergassy Universe) | Has Audiobook

Standalone (Vergassy Universe) | Has Audiobook

Cavalry Stories | Raconteur Press

Mecha Stories | Raconteur Press

Alternate WW II | Raconteur Press | Coming Sept 2024

Made in the USA
Coppell, TX
14 November 2025

63198755R00075